Fire At Midnight

VIVIAN SINCLAIR

Copyright

This book is a work of fiction. Names, characters, and incidents either are the product of the author's imagination or are used fictitiously. Any resemblance to actual persons, living or dead, or events is entirely coincidental.

Published by East Hill Books

Cover design: Vivian Sinclair Books

Cover illustrations credit:
© Pondshots | Dreamstime.com

ISBN-13: 978-1545410066
ISBN-10: 1545410062

To find out about new releases and about other books written by Vivian Sinclair visit her website at VivianSinclairBooks.com or follow her on the Author page at Amazon, Facebook at Vivian Sinclair Books, or on GoodReads.com

Maitland Legacy, A Family Saga Trilogy - western contemporary romances

Book 1 – Lost In Wyoming – Lance's story

Book 2 – Moon Over Laramie – Tristan's story

Book 3 – Christmas In Cheyenne – Raul's story

Wyoming Christmas Trilogy – western contemporary romances

Book 1 – Footprints In The Snow – Tom's story

Book 2 – A Visitor For Christmas – Brianna's story

Book 3 – Trapped On The Mountain – Chris' story

Summer Days In Wyoming Trilogy - western contemporary romances

Book 1 – A Ride In The Afternoon

Book 2 – Fire At Midnight

Book 3 – Misty Meadows At Dawn

Seattle Rain series - women's fiction novels

Book 1 - A Walk In The Rain

Book 2 – Rain, Again!

Book 3 – After The Rain

Virginia Lovers Trilogy - contemporary romance:

Book 1 – Alexandra's Garden

Book 2 – Ariel's Summer Vacation

Book 3 – Lulu's Christmas Wish

A Guest At The Ranch – western contemporary romance

Storm In A Glass Of Water – a small town story

CHAPTER 1

Twenty-five years ago, Santa Fe, New Mexico

"Dad, I'm hungry."

"You know better than to interrupt me when I am working, Nathan." His father stepped away from his easel, admiring his art, and added some extra touches with his brush. "Well, what do you think?" The question was addressed more to himself than to his seven year old son, who, in his opinion, had not inherited his artistic talent. A pity, but it could not be helped.

Little Nathan looked closer and shivered. In the center of the large canvas, there were three women in profile, their hair flowing in the back and their mouths open in a silent cry. Around their faces, there were swirls of black and red paint in an abstract background. "They are angry," Nathan said still shivering.

"Exactly. 'Anger' - this will be the title of the painting. I have the feeling that this painting will be the key to my success, paving my way from dusty Santa Fe to the den of art connoisseurs and auction houses, New York City." Like every artist, Simon Young dreamed of acquiring fame and name recognition in the art world.

"Why New York City? I like Santa Fe."

"Santa Fe is a good place to start as an artist, but fame... can only be achieved in New York City, where the art galleries are and where collectors don't think twice before paying thousands of dollars for a painting."

Nathan looked back at his father's painting. His father had told him many times that he was not artistically inclined, but he doubted that any person could enjoy waking up every day and looking at the hideous shouting women. Not even for free. Paying thousands of dollars for it, was ... probably not going to happen. "Ugly," he said before thinking and he bit his lip.

But his father was not mad at him this time. He smiled. "Yes. It's ugly, but it's also beautiful in its ugliness."

Only an artist could split hairs like that. There was nothing beautiful in his father's painting, he thought.

"What do you consider beautiful?" his father

asked him.

"I don't know. A sunny day with blue sky, flowers, the houses in Taos, the horse I rode in spring when you painted at the ranch south of here, the mesas…"

"Pshaw," his father scoffed. "That is vulgar beauty without emotion. A true artist needs to reveal the inner beauty of a powerful emotion."

Nathan had a nightmare that night. The three witches in his father's painting where chasing after him screaming their anger at him. He woke up sweating. His heart was racing. He called for his father, but he was not at home. Every evening, till late at night, Simon Young could be found at the sports bar in town, commiserating with other artists like him, who were yet to be discovered.

That night, Nathan understood that he had to find his own way in life or he'd go to bed hungry like he did then. His father was not a bad man, but he was unable to take care of a child and he was too immersed in his art to pay attention to his son.

His mother, a Native American from Oklahoma, had died giving birth to him. Her family didn't want him either.

So Nathan made his own way in life. He was athletic and he hoped to go to college on a football scholarship. When this didn't happen, and he was wondering how to get money for tuition, a recruitment center for the Marines offered him a solution.

When he told his dad that he had enlisted, the only answer he got was, "Good. It was about time you stood on your own two feet."

Fifteen years passed since he'd called the Marines his home. Nathan kept in touch with his father occasionally, but the gap between them was so wide that they didn't have much to talk about. And that suited them both.

Present time, summer in Laramie, Wyoming

The vivid dream came again. The teenager, a boy really, twelve or fourteen years of age, came closer to their army vehicle, smiling. Nathan saw his hand slowly inching to his belt. He grabbed his hand and pushed him away, and shouted at his men to get down. Then, there was only smoke, dust, and a searing pain in his abdomen, followed by darkness.

He woke up confused. His heart was pounding. He turned on the light on his nightstand and there she was, his guardian angel. Honey blond hair and big blue eyes. His Laura was smiling at him from the picture, representing all that was beautiful and innocent in this world. Reminding him why he'd fought for ten long years in far away countries.

The wedding party was going on strong. Sheriff McRavy was twirling his bride on the makeshift dance ring in his back yard. People were joking good-naturedly and having a great time. Considering the continuous row of people who'd stopped by during the day to congratulate the happy couple, you'd think the food and drinks on the long tables outside would have disappeared, but neighbors and friends alike brought new refreshments and the merriment and dancing continued long into the afternoon and evening.

Deputy Nathan Young was new in town and he didn't know many people. He liked that the locals were friendly and were trying to include him in their jokes and conversations. He was not talkative. It was not in his nature to tell the story of his life to the first unknown person that crossed his path. But he smiled and kept to the side, mostly observing what was going on.

He didn't dance much. His internal wounds were not completely healed, not even after three surgeries and a year of physical therapy.

He'd accepted the special invitation to the wedding mainly because Jack McRavy was his boss and friend, and Nathan respected him very much. He expected to be uncomfortable not knowing anyone in town. He was surprised that he enjoyed himself. It was a nice summer day and he discovered that it made him feel content and at peace to see happy people around him.

The sheriff had a nice property here and Nathan wandered away to admire the view. He was near the barn, debating if it would be an intrusion to peek inside at the horses, when he heard a soft cry, like a mewling inside. At first, he thought it was an animal in distress, but coming closer, he realized that there was a person crying inside. Maybe he or she wanted privacy. But what if it was a child in need of comfort? He'd seen children running and playing around the house. Who could be crying today when everyone was happy?

The door to the barn was cracked open and Nathan went inside. The noise came from one of the stalls. He walked in silence, checking the stalls. Three horses looked at him with curiosity and he patted their noses. Too bad he had no treat for them. He admired their healthy coat and bone structure. The sheriff had prime horse flesh.

The cry turned to sobbing and sniffing. Now certain that it was a child, Nathan pushed the last stall open. And he had the surprise of his life. Sitting on a bale of hay, was a petite, delicate woman, with honey gold hair, falling in waves past her shoulders down her back. It was partly covering her face, which was buried in the neck of a… Was that a goat? Yep. It was a white soft baby-goat that she was hanging onto for dear life.

Uncomfortable with the situation, but fascinated by the dark golden hair, Nathan asked her, "Listen, lady, can I be of any help? You look distressed."

Surprised, she raised her face to look at him. Nathan had never seen a more beautiful face. Although tears were running down her porcelain cheeks, her eyes were not red. Even her sniffy nose was not swollen, but elegantly upturned. A pink bow-arched mouth completed this beautiful image.

It was Nathan's turn to be shocked. "Laura," he whispered. Indeed, in front of him was the image that had accompanied him during the lonely nights, soothing him after his nightmares. The image of the perfect woman had come to life.

Careful not to scare her, Nathan came inside and sat on the bale of hay near her. She didn't run away. She looked at him with curiosity.

"How do you know my name?" she asked, in a soft, barely audible voice. "I'm sure I've never met you in my life. I'd have remembered."

Gently, Nathan wiped the tears off her face, marveling at the perfection of her features and the velvety skin. "I took your picture from our sheriff's desk. He told me your name."

The mention of the sheriff's name brought new tears in her eyes. "Why?" she asked between sobs.

"Because I've never seen such a beautiful picture in my life and I wanted it to remind me that not everything is ugly and bad in life," he answered with honesty. "I never imagined that the reality can be better than the picture," he said, touching her face again. This brought a tiny smile through tears. She thinks I'm joking – Nathan thought – she has no idea how truly beautiful she is. "Tell me why are you crying when everyone else is having fun, dancing and partying."

"Because…I messed up my life. First, I married young against my brother's advice. My ex-husband was a dashing police officer, tall and strong and his name was Jack. It wasn't long before he started beating me. My brother saved me, but I ran away to a women's shelter and left him to face prison, instead of going as a witness to tell what happened. I was battered and scared for me and my son, but I still blame myself for being a coward."

"You had reasons…"

"I left my brother Joe to face that monster alone. Then, last year, when Sheriff McRavy asked me on a date, I was afraid to say yes. I liked him very much, but he was a big man, a law officer, and his name was Jack. So I said no and I returned with my brother to Colorado Springs."

"All right. I understand. But why are you unhappy now?"

Laura sighed and leaned into him. Nathan placed his arm around her and let her rest her head on his shoulder. He inhaled the flowery smell of her hair. Sweet, like her. She didn't appear afraid of him and Nathan was a big man too, naturally tall, and beefed up by the intense training in the military.

"I returned here and I took the position of pediatric nurse at the hospital. Then, I looked for Jack, the sheriff. I thought we could…"

"I see. You thought that he'd be willing to date you and that he felt the same."

"Yeah, I thought he felt the same. I thought he understood that I was scared and that I needed time to process my feelings. Instead, he was engaged to be married and very much in love with another woman. How was this possible?"

How indeed? Nathan wondered. How could the sheriff prefer another woman to the beautiful Laura? Not that Dr. Iris Richardson was not a wonderful, capable woman. However, another question was more pressing. "Do you still love him?"

Laura blinked and thought about it. "You think I'm crying because I love him and I lost him? No. I didn't know him that well and we were not close enough for me to fall in love with him."

Nathan could have pointed out that you only need a moment to look at another person, or at a picture, and you can fall irrevocably in love. Love at first sight. It was possible. It was real.

"I am crying because I messed up another

opportunity in my life," she continued. "Jack is a good man and I like him. I'm sorry that I didn't give him… and us a chance. Instead, I ran away like a scared rabbit. Jack took my rejection hard at the time and he didn't deserve it. I came here today to assure myself that he is truly happy. He is and I'm glad, but looking at him dancing with his bride, I can't help but regret the lost chance for myself. It could have been me waltzing with him out there."

That's it, Nathan made up his mind. He stood up and extended his hand to her. "Ma'am, may I have this dance?"

"What? Here?" Laura looked around her in the small stall.

"No, of course not here. Out there, where everyone is dancing."

After hesitating a moment, Laura placed her hand in his and smiled. "Thank you, yes."

CHAPTER 2

In the beginning, Laura looked around embarrassed at the other people dancing.

"Just relax. Look at me and imagine you are with your ideal partner and you are the belle of the ball," Nathan told her. "The rest of the world disappears. Only you and your ideal man, the one who loves you above all else."

At first they moved awkwardly; neither one had much practice dancing recently. Then leaning into each other and finding a rhythm that suited them together, they turned round and round slowly, and Nathan felt Laura relaxing in his arms.

She looked up at him and smiled. "You have the advantage here because you know who I am. What is your name?"

"Nathan. I'm Nathan Young."

She stopped uncertain. "I think I know you. Aren't you the deputy who lives with TJ Lomax?"

It couldn't be helped. He was a law officer like

her abusive ex-husband. Was that going to scare her away? "Yes, I am," he admitted.

It didn't faze her. "I live next door at Mrs. Taylor. She watches over my son Joey when I'm at work. I'm a pediatric nurse at the hospital. I've seen you leaving for work in the morning when I come home from a night shift," she said smiling shyly, looking at him from under her long eyelashes.

"We're neighbors. A fortunate coincidence."

"It's not a coincidence. When I returned to Laramie, I came to see TJ Lomax. He was the only other person I could call 'friend' apart from Jack McRavy. TJ suggested that I could rent a room from Mrs. Taylor, next door. It worked out better than I expected. She's a wonderful person and quite lonely in her old age."

"So, moving back here was good for you."

Laura's eyes moistened with tears. "I don't know. I like my job and I can provide adequately for my son. That is a good thing. But when I finally got my courage up to talk to Jack, it was too late. He'd already moved on."

"Laura, Jack moved on, but all the single men this side of Wyoming would be at your feet if they knew you are available." Nathan caught her face between his palms. "Don't you know how beautiful you are?" Laura looked at him helplessly, so he added, "Unless you've decided that only Jack will do. Then it is hopeless, because he is very much taken."

They watched the newly married couple waltzing around, their love for each other obvious in their eyes.

Laura sighed. "No, I don't want Jack. It's just that… I don't know what to do with my life now. When I left Colorado Springs, I had a plan, a motivation. I knew what I wanted. Or so I thought. Now, I feel like a derailed train. I don't know if I am making sense."

He nodded. "Yeah, you are. I was in a similar situation recently. I was at a crossroads in life, undecided where to go next or what to do."

It was starting to get dark and the strings of lights were turned on all around the yard. Some people said their good-byes and left, although the party was still going strong.

"Let's go home," Nathan said, taking Laura's hand. "Did you come with someone?"

"No, I came by myself. At first, I couldn't decide if I wanted to come or not, but TJ convinced me. He said that I have to go on with my life too. And this is the best place and moment to start, realizing that it's time to make other plans."

"The old man was right as always. Let's go."

When he stopped his truck in front of Mrs. Taylor's house, Nathan knew he had to be honest with Laura.

"I'd like to see you again, Laura." Seeing that her face showed fear like a doe caught in the headlights, he hastened to assure her. "Of course, it will be your decision. I'll never pressure you in any way."

"All right then. I like you Nathan, but I don't know if I'm ready to trust any man again. I thought I was ready with the sheriff, but he didn't want me."

His face inscrutable in the darkness, Nathan continued to talk slowly, "I know you were afraid of Jack because, like your ex, he works in law enforcement and he has to deal with violence every day. Before Jack hired me as his deputy, I was in the Marines for fifteen years. Active duty, I fought against the enemy in combat. I've seen unspeakable things, violence, killing, death. I wanted you to know this."

She reached out to him, placing her smaller hand under his on the wheel. "You should be proud of serving in the military. What happened?"

"A bomb, a lot of pain, three surgeries, and a year of physical therapy," he explained succinctly, not wanting to terrify her with the real horror of what he'd been through in the past year. "Then I got a decoration and honorable discharge. Like you, I had no idea what to do with myself. Jack convinced me to stay here for the summer. I'm glad I did. I got to know you."

"I'm glad too," she whispered.

She was sweet, and Nathan had a hard time resisting the temptation to kiss her. But it was too early. He just touched her face and, like a kitten, she rubbed her cheek against his callused palm.

"Good night," she said and disappeared into the

house, leaving Nathan looking after her, smiling.

Two days later, the sheriff called Nathan to his office to talk about a deposition in court he had to do the next day.

"How is married life?" Nathan asked.

Jack grinned like a fool. "It couldn't be any better. With the right woman, it is pure bliss. Whoever invented the honeymoon was a genius. I strongly recommend it. You should go to the knitting ladies at the Cowgirl Yarn shop. They'll have you married in no time at all."

Nathan winced. Give him a ferocious band of Taliban fighters and he'd face them without fear, but the matchmaking sweet old ladies terrified him. Besides, his heart was already taken. "I found the perfect woman for me," he remarked mostly for himself.

Jack paused with his coffee cup in his hand. "Don't tell me you're serious about Laura."

"And what if I am?" Nathan bristled. "Are you warning me off?"

"No, of course not." Jack set his cup on his desk. "But I consider you my friend. Laura is beautiful and she has a feminine vulnerability and helplessness that appeal to us men. It makes us feel macho, strong, and protective. If you take away her outer shell, Laura is weak and unable to make decisions and follow through."

"I think you are too hard in your judgment of her character, perhaps because she refused to date you."

"Is that what you think? That the grapes are sour because I couldn't have them? You are wrong. Think about it, Nathan. What I said it's true. When times are difficult – and life is hard most of the time – you'll have to deal with a woman who is wringing her hands and crying, on top of the hardship. Is this who you want as your partner in life?" Jack raised his hand to stop Nathan's protest. "You don't have to answer. Just think about it."

Nathan went to the window and looked outside. It was a nice summer day. The storm was only in his heart. He knew that his friend was right in a way. That was how Jack perceived Laura. That was the image Laura herself projected to others. He knew all that, but unfortunately, it was too late for him. He'd fallen in love with a beautiful picture, and now that he'd met her in person, he could not let her go. Besides, he felt that under all that fragility, Laura hid unexpected strengths.

"Not all women are as strong as Dr. Richardson," he said finally, still looking out the window.

"McRavy. Dr. Iris McRavy," Jack corrected him with pride. "Yes, she is quite a woman, my wife. Strong and reliable. Beautiful and warm. She takes my breath away. I thank my lucky stars I met her."

"I just met Laura. I don't know what is going to happen. She might reject me as she did you. It is possible. But I'm going to be open-minded and try to get to know her. I bet there are more layers than you think. Laura had to endure terrible abuse and it's remarkable that she survived. No wonder she's traumatized. Don't judge her, Jack. She went through a lot."

Outside, a dusty truck stopped in front of the Sheriff's Department and two cowboys, one older around sixty, and one younger, about half his age, crossed the parking lot to the entrance. Their somber faces predicted trouble ahead for the department.

"You're probably right. As a police officer in Dallas, I've seen many cases of abuse. I could never understand why the battered women stayed with their abuser and sometimes even covered for him, not admitting what they suffered at their hands. It was frustrating. In my mind, after the first slap, they should have left without looking back. Why did they allow the abuse to continue and worsen?"

Nathan thought about it. Why indeed? "I guess sometimes they depend on the abuser to provide for them and their children. They don't have anywhere to go and are afraid to leave. Most of the time, they hope that the abuse will stop as promised by their partner. This is only a point of view from the outside. We'll never know what is truly going on."

Jack opened his mouth to answer when there was a knock on the door. Nathan turned to see the two cowboys coming in. It looked like Jack already knew them. Smiling, he rose and shook hands with them.

"John Monroe, it's good to see you again. I got a little sidetracked with the wedding and I forgot to ask you if you had more rustling."

"That's why I came by. I had some business in town and I came first to tell you that your wedding was the grandest we've seen in these parts. We're all happy that you married Dr. Richardson."

"She is Dr. McRavy now."

"You're right, of course," Monroe agreed readily. "But let me tell you why I wanted to see you."

"More rustling," the sheriff anticipated.

Monroe waved his hand. "Some. Not much. One cattle, here and there."

"Even one missing is one too many." Born and raised on a ranch, Jack McRavy knew how damaging it was to lose cattle.

"True. But now I have another issue to worry about."

"What is that?"

"Midnight fires," said the younger one, who until now had kept silent.

"As you know, our property neighbors the Richardsons'. I even bought some of his land when he became too old to work and he sold it," Monroe explained. "They are both quite isolated. Since the Richardsons' house burned, my men have seen camp fires at midnight in remote areas, near the canyon separating the two ranches."

Jack frowned. "That's not good. It's a dry summer. A spark or lightening can create a wildfire and we'll have a disaster on our hands."

"True. We tried to approach them to see what's going on, but by then the fire was only smoldering and had been extinguished. The camp was deserted. Very strange. It's like they were playing or using the fire as signals. My men are superstitious, what with all the local legends about the dead outlaws or Indians haunting the more remote places."

"Bah, they are just legends, that's all," Jack scoffed. "Next, you'll tell me that you believe aliens are plaguing your land." Monroe raised his eyebrows. "What? Don't tell me that is what you think?"

"Frankly, I don't know what to think. My men, all seasoned cowboys, cross themselves and refuse to ride there at night. I'm at the end of my wits."

Nathan, who had listened quietly to the conversation, stepped forward. "I could do it, Jack. I could camp there at night and see what's going on."

Monroe looked at him and Jack slapped his desk. "What was I thinking? Sorry, I forgot to make introductions. John, this is our newest deputy, Nathan Young. Nathan maybe you've met John Monroe and his sons at my wedding."

Nathan shook hands with the rancher, who had a firm grip and was still appraising him.

"I should go there at night," Jack said with some hesitation, probably not happy about abandoning his new bride every night for a stake out.

"I can do it, Jack," Nathan repeated.

Monroe had doubts. "I don't know. You are new at this job."

Jack felt he had to clarify. "Nathan is new at being a deputy sheriff, but fifteen years in combat, fighting Taliban and other terrorists, make him an expert."

"Is that so?" Monroe eyes widened as he looked at Nathan again.

Nathan hated to boast and to talk about his feats as a soldier. "Let's just say I had a lot of experience with guerilla warfare in enemy territory, including at night."

Monroe nodded. "Very well then. Thank you. I'll call you when I see anything suspicious. And thank you, Jack. The old sheriff would have laughed at me and dismissed my worries as unimportant."

CHAPTER 3

Thursday was meatloaf and mashed potatoes day at Kate's diner at the truck stop west of town, just off the highway. The diner was a rather seedy place, patronized by truckers attracted by Kate's good food and some locals down on their luck, attracted by the lower prices.

Kate was a middle-aged woman, tall and wide, who had no difficulty dealing with her more unruly customers.

One month ago, Deputy Young came to the truck stop to bring Kate the money stolen by a thief. It so happened that it was a Thursday, and Kate served him her famous meatloaf. Since then, Nathan had made a habit to visit the truck stop on Thursdays and enjoy the homemade food.

Usually, he took a seat at a booth in the back of the diner and savored the good meal at leisure. Once in a while, truckers sat opposite him in the booth, eating hurriedly, and telling Nathan stories from life on the road, or from life in general, if they were so inclined to unburden their heart and mind. Others preferred to make small talk, complaining about the weather or the roads' deplorable condition.

Nathan was a good listener. Not a talker himself, he listened to the people around him, making appropriate sounds in agreement and assuring them of his attention. Not that they cared if he listened or not. The solitude on the road made them in need of company and conversation, if only for the short time spent in the diner.

Today, it was a local who sat opposite Nathan in the booth. The local assumed that Nathan was a trucker driving through town. In order to make people more at ease around him, Nathan never wore his uniform when he was off duty.

"Good food," the local man said, mixing his mashed potatoes with the gravy. The result was an unappetizing mound that looked like mud. The man took a forkful and closed his eyes in ecstasy. "Mmm, good. You see, my wife passed away three years ago, and since then, I've been craving her meatloaf and mashed potatoes. I tried other places, but none tasted quite the same, until I found Kate's diner. This…," and he pointed to his half-empty plate, "…this is almost right and equally delicious to my Edna's. Did you try Kate's coconut and vanilla pie? It's out of this world good."

"No, I didn't. And I'm sorry for your loss," Nathan added politely.

The man paused and looked at Nathan, then at his plate. "Yeah, thank you. It is strange that we fought like cats and dogs all the time, but now that she's gone, I miss her very much." He wiped a tear from the corner of his eye. "When I'm at home, I expect she'll come after me shouting that I didn't fix the faucet in the bathroom or I left the lights on in the family room. But she's not there and no one is shouting." He sniffed and started eating again. "That's why I come here. Eating this food reminds me of her and makes me feel closer to her." After another pause. "Are you married?"

That was the most unusual conversation Nathan had in a long time, although between attacks, his brothers-in-arms used to remember moments spent with their families at home. "No, I'm not married."

"You should be. Life is too short to be spent alone."

"Do you have children?" Nathan asked him.

The older man nodded. "Two daughters. The eldest is married. She lives in Oregon, the other in Denver. Both of them asked me to move in with them. But I'm an old man. My house is here. My wife is buried here. I'd feel out of place moving into my daughter's house. I like to have my own space, with my things and my memories. Small as it is, it's mine. And I have a chicken in my coop, the only one left. I couldn't part with it. To do what? Go to Denver and live in a fancy condo. No, thank you. My place is nice and peaceful." He shook his head. "Although, to tell you the truth, I could do with better next door neighbors. These people bought the house a few years back, when Edna was still alive. Never-do-wells, the bunch of them. I heard they've been in trouble with the law. For a while, the house appeared abandoned and it was quiet. A couple of days ago, I had a premonition. I was feeding Belinda, my chicken, when I heard a dreadful motorcycle roar. Darn, I said to myself, Coyote is back in town. And sure enough, there he was, all his tattooed self. Belinda ran away into her coop and so did my peace of mind. Ran away."

Nathan had finished his meal and he left some bills on the table, ready to go. He'd listened to the old man's ramblings with half an ear. But the word Coyote resonated in his brain. What were the odds that it was the same biker who had terrorized the neighboring ranches? That one had left town over a month ago and good riddance. The portrait handed down to other sheriff's departments had been fruitless until now.

He rose to leave, then changed his mind. "My name is Nathan Young," he said extending his hand.

"I'm Good Old Bill. Bill Sanders. I had a carpentry business here in town." They shook hands.

"It was nice to meet you Good Old Bill. I'll be here to eat my meatloaf every Thursday. If you have a hankering to do the same, meet me here. And if you hear more about your pesky neighbor, I'd be grateful if you'd let me know."

The other one frowned. "Why would you be

interested in Coyote? Aren't you a trucker?"

"No. I'm a deputy sheriff. Let's just say, we've been interested to catch Coyote for quite some time. He's wanted for arson among other things. But we'd like to catch him in the act, otherwise Judge Fontayne will let him go with a small bail. Your help would be indispensable."

Good Old Bill straightened. "You mean, like doing my civic duty."

"Exactly so," Nathan answered and saluting, left the diner.

He parked his truck in the driveway, behind TJ's rusty truck, and got out whistling, anticipating a few enjoyable hours in front of the TV before going to bed. As it was his habit, he looked at the house next door, where Laura lived at Mrs. Taylor's. A boy, not much older than six, was sitting on the front steps, with a baseball bat and a glove in his hand. He looked unhappy and lost.

Usually, Nathan didn't interfere in other people's

family business, but there was something about the little boy that reminded Nathan of himself at the same age. He came closer and looked at the boy.

"Are you practicing?" Nathan asked the boy pointing to the baseball bat.

The boy looked at Nathan and shrugged. "Not really. I don't have anyone to play with."

"What about your classmates at school or friends?"

"I don't know them yet. We just moved here and I'll start school in the fall. I met some boys down the street and they don't want to play with me. They were mean and said I'm too small." He sniffed.

Oh yes. Kids could be mean and reluctant to accept a newcomer in their circle.

"They pushed me and kicked me," the kid continued.

Bullies. This could be a more serious issue. "Did you tell your parents?"

"I got no parents. It's only my mom and me. And she's busy working at her new job."

"What about your dad?"

The boy looked down at his baseball bat. "He was a bad man and they took him away."

So this must be Laura's little boy. What was he doing alone outside, talking to strangers? "Where is Mrs. Taylor?"

"Inside. She fell asleep on the couch, watching one of her movies."

Nathan took a seat on the top step near the boy. Talking at the same level made it more approachable. "You're Laura's son, Joey, aren't you?"

The boy nodded. He had the same big blue eyes with long lashes like Laura. "And you are the policeman living next door."

"I'm a deputy sheriff."

"Do you like it here, in this town? 'cause I hate it here. I miss my Uncle Joe and the other boys at school in Colorado Springs. Why did we have to leave?"

"Your mother needed a job in her specialty. But if you want, we could practice throwing and hitting the ball together. What do you say?"

"Really? You don't think I'm too small?"

"Yes, really. We'll start tomorrow afternoon. And don't worry, you'll grow tall. I was about your size at your age. At fourteen, I started growing and growing."

"That would be awesome," Joey said clapping his hands. "Have you always wanted to be a deputy sheriff?"

"No, I never imagined I'd be one. But life turned out this way. I was a Marine until recently."

"Wow! A Marine..." Joey's eyes sparkled with admiration. "Did you fight the bad guys?"

"More bad guys than I wanted... Now, about our practice. I'll come tomorrow afternoon when I finish work. Meanwhile try not to get into trouble with the mean boys."

The door opened and a harried Mrs.Taylor, holding a wrap tightly around her, came in the door. "Joey, there you are. You gave me quite a scare when I saw you were missing. You shouldn't go outside without telling me. Hello, Deputy! I'm glad he's with you."

"Yes, ma'am. We were talking about baseball. Now, it's late and almost dark. I'll come tomorrow after work to practice hitting the ball."

"Very good. Just as long as I know where he is. Joey is a fast one. His mother told me he vanished one night and she searched for him all night, only to find him asleep in the neighbor's shed."

Nathan smiled. Joey was a handful to raise.

CHAPTER 4

It was past midnight when the short tune played by his phone woke him up. He checked the caller ID. Monroe, John.

"This is Nathan," he announced briefly.

"Deputy Young, I'm sorry to wake you. I need help and I don't know whom to ask." Monroe seemed shaken.

Nathan rubbed his eyes. "Did you see anything suspicious? More fires?"

"No, not today. This is personal. My eldest son came home from Montana distressed that his wife left him. We had a fight and he rode away alone in the dark. I'm going after him, but I'd like someone reliable with me. I'm afraid for him. Can you come with me?"

"Of course. It will take me about 30 minutes to reach your house, no matter how fast I drive. Have two horses ready for me, with food, water, blankets - it's summer, but the nights are chilly – and a small first aid kit. And call me Nathan."

He hung up, and in no time at all, he was driving fast on the deserted streets and onto the county roads to the Monroe ranch.

He found Monroe, pacing agitated in front of his house, clutching his chest from time to time. Not a good idea to take him on a search mission at night. "The horse came back after I talked to you. Only the horse. My boy could be hurt out there. Let's go," the rancher said breathing hard and clutching his chest again. There were several men gathered in front of the house, looking at their boss.

"No. You called me to search for your son. Trust me to do it. I am going alone. I need three good horses, one for me, one for your son, and a packhorse," Nathan said with authority.

"I'll come with you, if you don't mind," a younger man said. "I know the land well and no matter how good a tracker you are, you need a guide who knows every inch of the land."

Nathan measured him up and down. Young, well-built, with stamina, and above all, not panicky like

Monroe. "Who are you?"

"This is my second son, Connor," Monroe explained.

"How many children do you have, Monroe?"

"Seven, all boys. Lord knows I had more worries with them than with a passel of girls."

"Seven?" Nathan wondered.

"You know, more men spread all over would have more chances to find my son." Monroe tried to argue with him.

"It would be a mess. We'll need searchers to look for the searchers and so on. Or maybe it's my army training   stay together, and don't spread around in order to stay safe," Nathan explained. "Let's go," he addressed the younger man, Connor, not giving Monroe more time to argue with him.

There was a full moon, so they were lucky to have some light and to see where they were riding, without Nathan having to turn on his army flashlight that he always carried with him. It did wonders in the dark and he was sure he'd need it later.

"He went that way," Connor pointed out to their left.

Nathan looked at the dark shade at the horizon. "Is that a mesa?"

"In this light, it looks like that, but it's a taller outcrop of large rocks. Behind it, there is a deep canyon, like a crack in the surface of the earth People are superstitious about going there, especially at night. Beyond that is the Richardson ranch. We bought most of their land when they sold it. Dad took on some debt, but it was worth it. The land is always worth it."

"I wouldn't know. I never owned anything of value. I was a Marine for fifteen years," Nathan said matter-of-factly, wondering what it would be like to have a home, land, family, and a place to belong.

They were advancing slowly in the dark, under the eerie, slightly greenish moonlight. From time to time, Nathan stopped and turning on his flashlight looked for traces or clues.

"Tell me about your brother. Why did he run away?" Nathan asked Connor, not because he was interested in other people's business, but to distract the younger man from thinking of the worst that could happen to his brother.

Connor sighed. "Ethan was fighting with Dad. You see, Dad likes to have things done exactly as he says, and what he says is law. Ethan doesn't have a rebellious nature. But being the eldest, he always bore the brunt of whatever we all did wrong. When he was eighteen, he left to go to college in Montana. Dad was upset. We have University of Wyoming here in Laramie."

"He wanted to stretch his wings," Nathan observed.

"Rightly so. I can't blame him. Then he went on and married a local girl and he only told Dad after the ceremony. There was no wedding party, only the exchange of vows in church. Dad was angry and told him a few choice words. Afterwards, Ethan remained in Montana. End of story, you'd think."

"No, life is not that simple."

"No, it's not. After a few years of marriage bliss

– or so I assume – Ethan's wife left him and he returned here. Dad should have accepted him peacefully and let bygones be bygones… But no, the old man had to crow every day and to tell Ethan 'I told you so', until Ethan couldn't take it anymore and after a particularly nasty fight yesterday night, he rode away into the night. You know the rest."

Nathan turned on his flashlight and studied the ground and the surroundings. He nodded satisfied. "We'll find him, don't worry. We're on the right track."

"Were you a scout or tracker in the army?"

"In the Marines. No. I was a Gunnery Sergeant."

Properly impressed, Connor opened his mouth to answer, when Nathan pointed to the outcrop of rocks. "Look there, a fire."

In the distance, a burning fire could be seen clearly in the darkness of the night, a thin thread of smoke rising up into the air.

"It will die down by the time we get there. We'll only find an abandoned camp," Connor said. "That is what happened before. The ranch hands are a superstitious bunch and swore they'd never go to investigate at night, because the place is spooky."

"It's always the same place?"

"No, not the same place, but the feel of something creepy persists everywhere in these abandoned camps."

"Not this time," Nathan said.

"How do you know?"

"I don't. I just feel the fire is of an earthly nature. Next time we'll find the persons who set the fires." Nathan grabbed Connor's bridle to slow him down. "Not so fast. I understand your eagerness to find your brother, but the horses need time to find their footing in the dark to avoid sliding into a hole and breaking a leg. We'll find him. Better tell me about yourself. How come you didn't leave the ranch? Do you get along better with your father?"

"Dad is a cantankerous old man. No one gets along with him. Especially after Mom moved to Cheyenne and left him to raise the children alone, all seven of us. He visits her there several times a year and he claims they get along fine, but... I have eyes to see.

After Zachary and Jon, the twins, went to college to Denver, I had to stay. For the land. I was born here and this is my land. I don't care if the old man will disinherit me as he threatened several times. This is my land. This is where I belong."

Nathan nodded. "Good for you. I wish I could say the same. I wish I knew where I belong. It looks like nowhere. I was born in Oklahoma, raised in Santa Fe, New Mexico, and lived wherever the Marines needed me to go. Nowhere feels like home."

"Ah, man. I'm sure you'll find it; your personal haven, your home."

The closer they came to the fire, the more merrily it was burning sending plumes of smoke into the air. Nathan had been right.

When they were close, a strong voice boomed, "Stay where you are. Don't come any closer. I'm armed."

"Ethan, you idiot." Connor dismounted fast and ran to the man behind the rock near the fire. Nathan followed pulling all the horses up the hill to the fire.

"How could you give us such a scare to ride into the night alone?"

The eldest Monroe brother was not quite as tall as Connor, but he was well-built. In the firelight, Nathan saw him shivering dressed only in a t-shirt. He grabbed a blanket from the pack horse and handed it to Ethan.

"Bless you," Ethan said wrapping himself in the blanket. "Fire or no fire, it is colder than a witch's …whatever."

"How could you leave dressed only in a shirt. Don't you know better? Regardless how warm the days are in summer, the nights are chilly here on the Laramie plateau." Now that he found his brother well, Connor became happy and talkative. "When your horse returned at the stable without you, we were so worried."

Warmed under the blanket, Ethan explained, "I saw the fire in the distance and I came closer carefully. I think this time I took them by surprise and when they finally saw me, one of them fired a shot on the ground right in front of my horse. It scared the horse who rose on his hind legs neighing and throwing me to the ground. I was dazed by the fall and by the time I gathered myself up, my horse had run home abandoning me and the camp was deserted. They left in haste and the fire was not entirely extinguished, so I could revive it to get some heat."

"Did you see them?"

"Not very well. They were four, I think "

"Not aliens," Connor joked.

"Definitely not. Unless the aliens had a regular hunting rifle."

Nathan was investigating the camp. There was a kerosene camping lamp, very useful and the fuel could be used as starter for the fire. He found also an empty tin cup on the ground near the fire. It was clean. Nathan filled it with the now cold coffee from the bottle on the pack horse. He heated it up and handed it to Ethan.

"Drink it. It will warm you up." Then he brought three wrapped sandwiches and gave two to the brothers.

"Oh, man, this is good," Ethan moaned after several sips of the hot coffee.

"Mmm, you'd think we haven't eaten in a long

time," Connor muttered his agreement.

Ethan looked at Nathan with curiosity. "You're a newly hired man?"

Connor slapped his own forehead. "How could I be so dimwitted? Ethan, this is Deputy Sheriff, Nathan Young. He came to help discover who is behind the midnight fires."

"When you finish eating could you please show me where the shot was fired? Maybe I'll be lucky and find the bullet," Nathan asked Ethan.

"Sure. It nicked that reddish stone down there."

Nathan found the bullet after some searching. Looking around, he found that three men, not four had run away and at a distance from the rocks, they climbed into a truck and sped away.

"What could be in that direction?" he asked the brothers pointing to his right, somewhere in the distance.

"Nothing," Connor answered wiping his mouth. "Unless you count the makeshift bridge that crosses over the canyon to the Richardsons' ranch. But as I said the house is vacant now. The Richardsons are old, retired, and they moved to town to be closer to their granddaughter, Iris."

"Mmm, the one that married the new sheriff," Ethan added.

"Our sheriff," Connor corrected him.

Nathan nodded. "I know. I was at the wedding."

"There. So you know. Let's go home," Connor concluded.

CHAPTER 5

Laura was walking in the hospital hallway to the newborns room. She was tired, but happy. The little boy, brought by his parents with a wound that didn't heal, didn't have the flesh-eating bacteria as the doctor feared at the beginning. The infection had responded to antibiotics and the boy was sleeping peacefully now.

"Laura," she heard a baritone voice calling her name. She turned and froze. It was Dr. Jones, a thoracic surgeon, feared by all medical personnel, nurses and younger doctors as well. He was a wizard in the operating room, making miracles possible in difficult cases, but he was also famous for his explosive temper. Laura personally had seen a nurse crying because Dr. Jones had thrown on the floor the instruments she'd handed him, claiming that was not what he'd asked for. He'd called the nurse incompetent and other hurtful words.

Then, she heard one of her co-workers, a pretty nurse from cardiology, speaking with another at the cafeteria about Dr. Jones. It seems that the younger surgeon, Dr. Kovacek, adored by all the nurses, was in the operating room, performing a routine operation on the esophagus, when he discovered a tumor that was unexpected. He had no idea how big it was or if it was cancerous. He was in uncharted territory.

It was not very clear who called Dr. Jones, but the door opened and he entered like a dragon puffing smoke through his nose. "Who paged me?" he asked looking menacingly at young Dr. Kovacek.

"N-not me, sir," Dr. Kovacek answered stuttering, not daring to ask Dr. Jones' opinion about the patient on the table.

"See that you don't do it again," Jones said, leaving the room.

Luckily for the patient, Dr. Kovacek was also a very good surgeon, even if not as flamboyant like Jones. Quietly he cut more than was planned, removed the tumor, and the patient recovered well.

Laura had also been warned that Dr. Jones was recently divorced and was on the prowl for pretty young women. Dr. Jones probably expected women to fall at his feet, but actually, the reverse was true, women ran far away when they saw him in the hospital.

No wonder Laura froze when she heard his voice. "It's Laura, isn't it? I'm Dr. Jones," he said with a wolfish grin, meant to be charming.

"Yes, I know," Laura answered, paralyzed by fear. Wasn't there a rule that forbade co-workers to date? Probably not. Her first instinct was to run away. The sheriff, who'd wanted to date her last year, was a pussy-cat compared to this predator. Then she raised her chin in defiance. No more running. Her abusive ex-husband was in jail and this was her dream job. No one would chase her away.

Jones was not aware of her thoughts. His grin widened. "So you heard of me. Well, I didn't hear much about you, except that you are new in our hospital. I'd like to hear more, perhaps we could have lunch together."

Some people when cornered have strange reactions. That's what happened to Laura. Giving him a wobbly smile she said, "That would be great. I was supposed to meet my fiancé for lunch, but I'll tell him to join us. The more the merrier."

Jones frowned. "I thought you were divorced."

"Yes. I divorced my ex four years ago for being abusive."

"And you already have a fiancé here in town? I thought you had just moved here from Colorado."

"I've been here before, in the past year. I've known him for a while." She crossed her fingers behind her back.

But Jones didn't give up so easily. "Who is he?"

"He is Deputy Sheriff Nathan Young."

"Hmm, deputy sheriff, you say. All right." And he turned to go back to the elevator.

"Hey, what about that lunch?" After this impulsive question, she bit her lip. What possessed her to goad him instead of leaving him be?

"I just remembered I have a meeting. But make no mistake, I'll be watching you," he said before disappearing behind the elevator closed doors.

It sounded ominous, even a threat, but Laura had lived for a long time from one respite into the next. Worrying about what disasters the future would bring was counterproductive.

Unfortunately, she had to worry about another unexpected issue. Gossip spread news like wildfire in a small town. An hour later her new coworker Emmy told her, "Lucky you. Freshly arrived in town and you caught that yummy deputy sheriff. Couldn't you set your sights on Brett Lockhart? Nobody wants him."

"Well, we just…" What could Laura say? That they'd just met at the Sheriff's wedding? She was in trouble.

"When is the wedding?" Emmy asked.

Definitely, she was in big trouble.

Nathan came home a little late, after he talked to Jack McRavy about the fires at the Monroe's ranch. He was very tired. He parked his cruiser in the driveway and when he climbed down, he saw a scuffle at the other end of the street.

Tired as he was, he walked there to see what was happening. A small boy was cornered near a fence and four older boys were pushing him and kicking him. He was swinging wildly at them, cursing and yelling, until his fist connected with the soft abdomen of the biggest boy who seemed to be the leader of the four. He doubled over, while the others looked at him waiting for orders what to do.

"Grab him," he spat, still trying to catch his breath.

One tried to catch him, but the little one stepped back. Unfortunately, surrounded by them, he had no chance to get away. They caught him. He was twisting and pulling, trying to escape the hold.

The bigger boy came closer and raised his fist prepared to hit him, when Nathan intervened.

"Enough," he said quietly, grabbing the leader's wrist in midair. "I could ask you if you're not ashamed to attack a boy smaller than all of you. Four of you against one. But I think I'd be wasting my breath. You all obviously don't see anything wrong with this picture. So,

I'll tell you in the only language you understand. Touch him again, and I'll make you sorry. I'll see you all in juvenile court. That is a promise. Now beat it. I don't want to see you again."

They scattered immediately and Nathan went down on one knee to look at Joey. He had a bruise on his cheek that was turning blue rapidly and had scrapes all over. He opened his arms. "Come here, Tiger."

The little boy threw himself at Nathan, shaking with sobs and releasing the pent up fear that he held inside. Nathan squeezed him gently. "It's all right. You're too small to battle the dangers of the world alone. Let's go home to clean your war wounds."

Joey looked at him through tears. "Please, don't tell mama. That they attacked me almost daily, that I hate here, and I miss our home in Colorado Springs and my Uncle Joe. She endured a lot and now she's happy with her new job here. I don't want to upset her. I am all she has and I have to protect her."

It was like the whole world weight was on his small shoulders and Nathan had to do something. "Joey, listen to me. Bullies are everywhere, including in Colorado Springs. You've been lucky not to meet them there."

"Why were they mean? I didn't do anything to them," the boy asked.

"It's the way life is, the good and the bad. That's why we have law enforcement officers, to catch the bad ones. It is summer vacation and most kids are at home, working on the ranches or in summer camps. But I can take you to meet good boys your age and when school will start in the fall, you'll have already a lot of friends."

"Promise?"

"You've got my word. Now let's go clean you up and then we can throw some ball."

Laura found them in the evening, in TJ Lomax' small back yard eating hotdogs grilled by TJ and drinking lemonade. The sun was setting and the sky had a reddish hue, but the air still retained the warmth of the day. It was bound to be cool at night.

"Hello boys," Laura said taking a seat on the

wrought iron chair. Her feet hurt after a long day of standing and running from one patient room to another. But she was content with work well done. The little boy with an infected wound was recovering. "What happened to your face Joey?" she asked her son, who sported a purple bruise on his cheek.

It didn't escape her that Joey looked at Nathan before answering. And it was Nathan who answered, "Boys playing ball. It happens."

And Joey nodded vigorously, bobbing his head up and down. "Yeah. It happens."

Very well. Let them have their own little secrets. Laura stretched her feet and closed her eyes, inhaling the sweet smell of the flowering vines that covered the fence. It occurred to her that only a year ago she'd be worried about what happened to Joey and highly suspicious of the man in his company, in this case Nathan.

And now, somehow she was sure that Joey had nothing to fear from Nathan and the deputy would always protect the boy from harm. She was sure of it. She'd come a long way from the scared rabbit, who feared all men, to the woman trusting… well, not all men, but this particular one. She trusted this weathered soldier, who had seen violence and death, yet who was so gentle with her son.

"Tell me about your life in the Army."

"Marine, I was a Marine. And I think perhaps we should postpone this conversation. Joey is sleepy and needs to go to bed," Nathan said, stacking up the empty plates.

"No, I'm not sleepy," Joey replied his eyes fluttering closed.

"I'll carry him, next door to his bed," Nathan offered.

"Thank you. We need to talk. Could I come after Joey is asleep?"

"Of course. I'll wait for you here, later." Nathan picked up Joey, wincing when his torn abdominal muscles protested, and walked next door with the boy in his arms.

CHAPTER 6

Nathan was tired and the summer night was so peaceful, he thought he'd fall asleep right there, sprawled in TJ's garden chair. It was quiet, not even the crickets disturbed the silence of the night. Now and again, he heard only a late car in the distance with a noisy exhaust. He leaned his head backwards and looked at the myriad of stars in the dark sky. It was the most peaceful moment he'd had in a long time, probably in years.

The gate opened and Laura entered the back yard. She was delicate and walked gracefully. She was perfect and her beauty took Nathan's breath away like it did when he'd first seen her picture on the sheriff's desk.

"For fifteen years, I had a rough life fighting in far away places. When I saw your picture on the Sheriff's desk, I was struck by your beauty, the perfection of your features and more than that, it was the softness and kindness in your smile. It was everything that I didn't have in all the years of fighting. I took the picture from him and I kept it with me, on my nightstand, to look at it after my nightmares."

Slowly, Laura sat in the chair next to his. "I am not perfect, you know… Far from it. I'm a weak, scared woman, who had no courage to stand up to her abusive husband and to come back to defend my brother after running away. Don't put me on a pedestal, Nathan. See the real me, imperfect and weak as I am. Only then we might have a chance together," she told him with sadness.

He thought of what she said. "Jack told me a lot about you. I think he is a bit resentful for being rejected."

"I'm sorry."

"Stop being sorry for doing what was best for you at the time. You can't apologize for every little thing, for living and breathing, just because you think people might be offended. They'll survive. Look at Jack, how happy he is with Iris and how well his life turned up to be." He wiped the tears from the corner of her eyes. "And stop being sad and crying for every little thing." He grinned at her. "About us, my mind is set. I'm sure I can change your mind too. I'm a Marine. I'm not giving up."

"Did you like being a Marine?" Laura asked with curiosity.

Did he? Nathan asked himself. "It was a way of life. I enlisted at seventeen when I finished high school, and that was my life for the next fifteen years. At the beginning, I chafed at the enforced discipline. The rigorous training didn't bother me, but I resented being ordered. Later I got used to it. In fact, I embraced it because discipline is crucial in combat."

"Did you want to enlist when you were only seventeen? I mean, did you want to be independent, to see the world?" Nathan hesitated answering and Laura hastened to tell him, "Sorry if my questions are too personal. You don't have to answer. I just wanted to know if you resented the parental authority and wanted to be free for a change."

"No, not me. On the contrary, I was independent ever since I was a little boy. My father rarely remembered he had a son. He was an artist and his painting was all he cared about. I was on my own. I got involved with some wild kids in my senior year of high school. We all want to be accepted and to be part of a group."

"Oh, I see. The wrong crowd. Did they do drugs?"

"No, no such things. But we thought it was cool to spray paint the principal's house."

Laura smiled. "That was a prank."

"Yeah, a prank. Unfortunately, the principal didn't think it was funny, neither did the police he called, nor did the judge who explained to us that vandalism is a crime. Some of us got to do community service; others had to serve a few months in juvenile detention."

"Ouch."

"The judge said that the Army would make men out of us. A friend of mine asked him - if we enlisted, was our record going to be clean? If we do it right away, yes – the judge answered. And the rest is history. Both of us enlisted. I had a second motivation. I knew there was no money for me to go to college. The recruiter assured me that I could get a degree while in service. I became a Marine. My friend was more adventurous and became a

Navy Seal."

"What happened to him?" Laura asked genuinely interested in Nathan's story.

Nathan sighed. "He died seven years ago near Kandahar. Of the two of us, he was the one who never regretted that impulsive decision to enlist. Being a Navy Seal fit him like a glove. He loved every minute of his life."

"What about you?"

"I didn't regret it, no. But I had moments when I questioned that decision. When we lost our innocence and our trust in fellow humans because we have to expect that even a young boy can be an instrument of evil."

She touched his hand. His kind, compassionate Laura. "I know you were wounded…"

"Yeah. The doctors were amazed I survived. Three surgeries and a year of rehabilitation. And all this time wondering what to do with the rest of my life. I have an associate degree in engineering, but all I know is to be a Marine."

"And an excellent deputy sheriff. Everybody in town thinks so." Laura said firmly. Which reminded her of the conversation she had with her co-worker. No matter how much she dreaded, she had to confess to Nathan what she had done. It was not the kind of dread she felt when she knew her ex-husband would be angry with her. That awful feeling of dread doubled by paralyzing fear. This time she felt only a natural embarrassment that she had to involve him in the town's gossip, in order to avoid a man that made her uncomfortable.

"I have to confess something," she blurted out before changing her mind. "Today Dr. Jones stopped me in the hallway. He's our thoracic surgeon and the entire hospital staff fears him. He wanted to go to lunch with me, to get to know me better, he said. And I…" She stopped to take a deep breath.

"What? Was he impolite? Did he take liberties with you? Tell me."

"No, not at all. It's just that…" How could she explain the fear that came over her every time a man became too familiar or came too close? Laura blinked. All men, except Nathan. Tough Marine that he was, it didn't scare her at all when he came closer. On the contrary, she felt protected. "There is something about Dr. Jones that is scary. Maybe the fact that he looks at every woman with superiority, like a cat ready to pounce on a mouse. I don't like him and I'm lucky that I don't work with him."

"You don't have to go to lunch with him if you're uncomfortable," Nathan said patting her hand.

"No, I'm not going. But in that moment, I was shocked that he'd asked me, and I didn't know how to escape."

"A simple 'No, thank you' would have sufficed."

"I told him that I had to meet my fiancé."

"What fiancé?"

"That's the problem, I don't have one. So when he asked me who was my fiancé, I told him it was you." Laura told him agitated and embarrassed.

A slow grin bloomed on Nathan's face. "Good thinking."

"You don't understand. The gossip in this town spreads so quickly that in the afternoon, my co-worker, Emmy, asked me how I succeeded in such a short time to catch the most yummy deputy sheriff in town."

Nathan's grin widened. "Yummy, huh?"

"You won't be smiling when you hear she asked me when the wedding is going to be. This is a small town. The gossip grows and grows. One person says she's seen us together, the next says we're already engaged."

"I don't mind, if you don't." Gently he cupped her face, marveling at the velvety porcelain skin. Her eyes glittered like two sapphires in the dark, but she didn't pull back from his touch. She was like a curious kitten. Maybe she had never been touched with gentleness. Tentative at first, he touched her lips and was lost in her sweetness. He gathered her closer to him. She made some mewling sounds and he realized she was not protesting or straining away from his touch. On the contrary, she answered his passion trying to get closer to him. In that moment, Nathan realized that this was it.

This was the haven that he'd searched for so long. With Laura in his arms.

CHAPTER 7

The diner was noisy and the meatloaf was as good as always. Nathan ate it 'con gusto', keeping an eye on the door for Good Old Bill. After he finished his meatloaf, he ordered a slice of the coconut and vanilla pie.

Nathan was ready to pay for his meal and leave, thinking the old carpenter was not going to show today when he entered the diner looking around. He made a beeline for the booth and took a seat, placing his Stetson on the table.

The server placed in front of him a plate filled with Today's Special.

"Eat first. I'll wait," Nathan told him smiling.

"I was late today because my daughter from Denver called to tell me that she's taking two weeks vacation and she's coming to see me," Good Old Bill explained between forkfuls of the savory meatloaf.

"Aren't you glad that she's coming?"

"Of course I am. But I'm afraid of my neighbors,

Coyote and his partners. And I'm not much of an informant to you." He coughed and took a sip of the iced tea. "I tried to listen to what they were saying. I couldn't hear much. Their yard is full of trash, not a pleasant garden with trees and flowers like mine. They come outside only when they want to grill burgers. I went close to the fence to hear what they were saying, but I stepped into an empty bucket and made a lot of noise. This and the burnt burgers sent them indoors quickly."

Nathan could barely contain his laughter. "It's okay. You did your best."

"I heard one of them saying, 'We'll search again in the canyon' and Coyote saying 'I have the map'. Now what map do you think he was talking about and why does he need one when everyone has a GPS in his phone and knows how to use it?"

"Good question. I have to think about it," Nathan said, wondering what were the odds that Coyote was involved with the mysterious fires at midnight on the Monroe ranch. It was an idea worth investigating. "You did well. You might have given us an important clue," he told Good Old Bill.

Loud voices at another table interrupted their conversation. "The traffic was detoured around Omaha, I tell you…"

"Ha, no way. I was there this morning and there was no detour."

"Are you calling me a liar?"

Two truckers rose from their table, confronting each other. They were not drunk. Kate served no alcohol in her diner, not even beer. Kate herself came from the kitchen to see what the ruckus was about.

Forgetting that he was off duty and not in uniform, Nathan rose from his seat, got between the two truckers, and said, "Cool off you two or take your fight outside. This is a civilized place where friendly people come to enjoy Kate's food."

The taller one looked at Nathan dumbfounded. The shorter one swung his arm intending to hit the other in the face. Because he was shorter, his fist hit his opponent in the belly, causing him to grunt and look at the shorter one incredulously. Then the taller one narrowed his eyes and like an enraged bull bent his head forward threateningly. The shorter man recognized the danger, and he turned to run, squealing loudly.

The taller one hastened to run after him, but Nathan grabbed his arm. Looking in the angry man's eyes, Nathan spoke slowly to penetrate the other's enraged fog. "There will be no fighting now. Sit down and eat your meal."

The tall trucker understood authority when he heard a command. "But he hit me."

"Don't worry. I'll have a word with him too."

The trucker nodded. "All right." Just like that, he took his seat at the table and resumed eating. Then he paused and looked at Nathan. "You must have been in the Army."

"Marines. I was a Gunnery Sergeant," Nathan admitted.

The trucker saluted and continued eating.

The door opened and the short man entered. Encouraged that no one had followed him outside, he returned with a fighting gleam in his eyes. But after one look from Nathan, he retreated without protest.

When Nathan came back to his booth, Good Old Bill smiled at him, "Well done, Deputy."

Nathan opened his mouth to argue, but the old carpenter raised his hand to stop him. "Yes, you were a Marine, but make no mistake about it, today you confronted the two yahoos in high spirits because you felt that as a deputy sheriff you had too keep order in this county. So," he raised his iced tea glass. "Well done."

Next day, Nathan went to see the sheriff. Jack McRavy was sitting at his desk looking at a picture of his wife, with a goofy smile on his face. Baker, his little dog, raised his head to look at the newcomer.

"I see the honeymoon is still on," Nathan observed, extending his hand for Baker to sniff. "And why is your dog here?"

"Garrett is spending a few days of his summer vacation at the Gorman ranch, with his new friends, Wyatt and Billy, the older Gorman brothers. He loves it there, the animals, the horses, riding."

Nathan lowered himself gingerly into the chair in front of the sheriff's desk. His abdominal muscles, or whatever was left of them, hurt like crazy. Too much effort throwing ball with Joey the previous day. "I wanted to talk to you about that."

Jack blinked. "About what?"

"About Garrett and his friendship with the Gormans."

"You have objections?" Jack asked surprised.

"No. Of course not. On the contrary. I have a big favor to ask." He paused, not used to asking favors from anyone. But it needed to be done. "You know Laura has a little boy, six or seven years old."

Jack stiffened when he heard Laura's name. "Are you still a dreamer in love with a pretty face, without seeing the empty shell inside?"

"Jack, my friend, you told me your opinion of her, and I listened and considered it. It's strange, but Laura herself warned me about this. She said that, like all the others, I see only her beauty and not the woman inside. I know she's vulnerable and scared sometimes, but she went through terrible abuse at the hands of a man who should have cherished her. I also feel her strength. She is a wonderful mother who does her best to provide for her child, and a woman, who still has passion, despite being almost beaten to death. So, Jack, I respect your opinion, but please, in the future, refrain from criticizing Laura, or I'll have to hit you and I don't want to do that. You're my friend and my boss."

Jack set his wife's picture back on the desk. "O-kay… It's just that I want you to be careful. There is a rumor in town that you are engaged to Laura. So be careful. This is a small town. They'll have you married in no time at all."

"Yes, I know. Laura started the rumor unintentionally. She was being pressured with unwanted attention from a coworker. In order to avoid him, she told him she is engaged to me."

"That is exactly the kind of situations in which Laura gets herself embroiled."

"It's not her fault that she's beautiful. Men flock to her like bees to honey," Nathan bristled. "Let me tell you the truth, Jack. I intend to marry Laura. I'll take my time so that we can get to know each other and so that she can understand that I'd rather cut off my arm than harm her. But I will marry her. My mind is made up. This was not a spur of the moment decision. I thought about it very well."

"But why?" Jack asked genuinely puzzled. "I know she's beautiful, but a man needs more in life."

"She is exactly what I need, softness, a tender heart, gentle hands, warm smile. Everything that I've always craved in life and I never had. I want her in my life."

Jack rubbed his eyes, put his glasses on, then blinked and took them off. "All right. If that's what you want. Now, tell me what favor you wanted to ask."

"Laura has a little boy. Joey is skinny and small for his age. Like Laura, he went through a lot, and didn't have a real place to call home. He liked Colorado Springs, adapted there, and he loved his Uncle Joe. I don't know him, but listening to Joey, you'd think the sun rises with this Joe."

"Yeah, I know him. Just Joe. He worked as ranch hand at Diamond G ranch. Tom Gorman liked him a lot. After Laura's ex-husband was put in jail, he and Laura decided to return home to Colorado Springs. Joe was a good guy. Honest and reliable."

"I found four older boys cornering Joey and bullying him a couple of days ago. They were hitting him."

"We don't allow bullying in this town."

"Great. Unfortunately, it happens all the time everywhere. I'm afraid little Joey projects the kind of image that attracts bullies. Small, unable to defend himself, and easy to rile. I want to ask you if Garrett, who is about the same age, could introduce him to other boys, so that when school begins in the fall, Joey will not feel so alone and miserable."

"What a great idea. Why don't you bring him to my house this weekend to meet Garrett and the two Gorman boys?"

"Thank you, Jack. It was not easy for me to ask you, but I felt sorry for Joey."

"Then it's settled. Now, let's talk business. Any news about the aliens?"

"What aliens?"

"You know - the fires at midnight on the Monroe land."

Nathan rubbed his aching abdomen. "They exist in reality. Monroe didn't send us after imaginary fires. Of course, they are set by humans, who are doing, whatever they are doing there, at night, in secret. Technically, they are trespassing, so they have to do it in secret."

"Why are these things happening in my county?" Jack complained.

"Life would be boring otherwise."

"We could stake out the place and surprise them in the act."

"We could if they made their fire in the same place."

"Are you telling me they burn all of Monroe's land?"

"Not all. His property is pretty large. Only here and there, mostly along the canyon."

"Oh Lord, we'll have a wildfire in this dry weather."

"To give them their due, whoever they are, they extinguish the fire carefully when they leave." Nathan looked down at Baker who came to him. Obligingly, Nathan scratched him behind his ears. "Joey needs a dog for company."

"Don't tell my wife. In no time at all, Iris will fill your house with all the stray animals from the veterinary clinic."

CHAPTER 8

Friday morning, Nathan got a call from the sheriff.

"I'm in court, waiting for Judge Fontayne. Knowing him, I'll be tied here all morning. Iris' grandfather called me because he thinks someone is trespassing on his property, at his old ranch. As I said, I don't have time today of all days, to see what he wants. Could you please talk to him and see what the problem is?"

"Of course, Jack. I'll go there to see. Don't worry."

"Thanks. I have to go now."

Iris' grandparents had moved to town. They were old, almost eighty years old, and it was better for them to be near a medical facility if they needed one, and to be closer to Iris and Jack. Their old ranch was nearby, about thirty minutes drive, but it was isolated. As they were getting older, they had sold most of the land. Only the old house and some surrounding acres, maybe a hundred, remained of their property. And they intended to sell that too.

He tried calling rancher Richardson at the number Jack had given him, but it went straight to voicemail. What to do? He left a message that he was going to the ranch house to investigate.

He climbed into his patrol car and made a detour to the nearest gas station to fill his tank. While he was pumping gas, another cruiser belonging to the Sheriff's Department drove by and stopped on the other side of the pump. Deputy Brett Lockhart got out of the car. Oh joy! It was Nathan's lucky day. Since their last confrontation, Lockhart had steered clear of him and only talked to Nathan when it was absolutely necessary for work related issues. Nathan liked it that way. It made both of their lives easier.

Unfortunately, today Lockhart decided to make an exception. He came closer to Nathan and put his sunglasses on. "Deputy Young, fancy finding you here."

"And why not?" Nathan muttered, praying his tank would fill up faster.

"Are you going to the office?" Lockhart asked, adjusting the pump hose that was coiled.

"No," Nathan answered curtly.

A sparkle of interest lit up Lockhart's eyes. "You got a lead about some mischief going on?"

"No, I don't." That reminded Nathan to call the dispatcher and let her know that he was going to the Richardson's ranch to check on the vacant house at the request of the owner.

Finally, his tank was full and the pump stopped. He nodded in the general direction where Lockhart was cleaning his window of what a bird had left him there, and then Nathan drove away.

He called Richardson's phone again and it went directly to voicemail. Nathan feared he was going on a wild goose chase. But then, why not? It was not like an abundance of crime afflicted the county. Lockhart was just waiting for the opportunity to jump into the fracas and was disappointed that everything was quiet.

Weather was nice. Summer was proving to be warm, but not unpleasantly so, here in southeastern

Wyoming. Nathan took his time to admire the vast spread of the high plateau.

The ranch house was isolated. From state route 30, he had to drive on secondary roads and country roads before reaching the old ranch house.

"Wow!" he said climbing down from the cruiser. The house was picture perfect. Nestled near some big boulders, the house was protected from winds and harsh weather and there were even some trees growing nearby. He could see a small vegetable garden to one side, which had been recently destroyed and abandoned. Tire tracks were crisscrossing it.

The dwelling was made of wood and stone. Although small, it looked nice. It could easily be enlarged by adding more living space. There was an old rusted truck parked nearby, but Nathan couldn't be sure if it was abandoned with the house or if anyone was there.

The door was closed, but not locked. It opened easily when Nathan turned the knob. "Anybody here?" he asked. No one answered, but he knew as soon as he stepped inside the large living room, empty of any furniture, that everything was not right. Yes, it was quiet, but a weird sort of silence, warning of danger.

He looked at the massive stone fireplace that covered an entire wall. The hook above the mantel, where the rancher had hung his Winchester, was now empty. It was likely that Richardson had taken the rifle with him when he'd moved out.

Nathan was startled by a loud cracking noise. He turned, instantly taking his gun out of the holster. Flashbacks from the past flooded him. Vacant, half demolished houses that were hiding places for Taliban militants, with the enemy springing from the most unexpected places.

In the cozy country kitchen, a window was open and it slammed closed with the same cracking noise. It was unnerving and Nathan blinked. The wind opened the window again and Nathan closed it quietly, trying to lock it shut. The lock had been broken. Richardson was right. Someone had broken into his house.

Nathan placed his gun back in the holster, but

kept his hand on it. There were several doors opening from the kitchen. He opened the first one on his right, and entered a long hallway with several open doors, leading to the bedrooms. Nathan listened, but there was only silence. Slowly, he returned to the kitchen and tried the next door. It was a pantry with some cans and jars.

It was an old unspoken agreement among ranchers in these remote places to leave shacks far on the range, or vacant houses, supplied with basic foods in case some poor cowboy got lost in bad weather or late at night. It was a law of survival.

Nathan closed the pantry door. He went to open the next door. A staircase descended into the darkness below and a musty smell hit him. It looked like a cellar. Nathan had no desire to meet some rats, so he was ready to close the door, when a sound of distress broke the silence of the house. It came from the cellar. He searched for the light switch and turned on the light. There was only a low wattage bulb hanging above the stairs, but it was enough to see a dark shape sprawled at the base of the stairs. Nathan checked the door first, so as not to get locked in the cellar accidentally. There was no lock on the door. He propped it wide open and made his way down the stairs. Old man Richardson was laying there unconscious.

Nathan checked him for wounds. He had a swollen goose egg at the back of his skull. "Mr. Richardson, can you hear me?"

The rancher moaned. Nathan supported him under one arm and succeeded to lift him up. The rancher was old and frail, but Nathan did not have enough strength in his torn abdominal muscles to carry him upstairs. Together, step by step, they made their way up into the kitchen. There, Richardson collapsed in a sitting position on the floor.

"Did you see him?" Nathan asked him.

The rancher was rather shaken. "No. He hit me from behind. Go look for him. He must still be here."

"I can't leave you here alone."

"Sure you can. What's he going to do? Hit me again?"

That and more, if he was a killer – Nathan

thought, but he didn't argue with the hurt old man.

The house was silent, except for the window with the broken lock. His instinct told Nathan that the house was truly empty. That left the barn.

Again, the barn doors were open, although there were no animals. Quietly, Nathan stepped inside. No noise.

He looked inside the stalls. They were empty. Nothing here. He was ready to leave when the same instinct that had saved him during years fighting guerilla on the streets in Iraq or in the mountains of Afghanistan, raised the small hairs at the back of his neck. Danger.

He jumped to the side, right in time to see a sharp knife striking the post near the stall door where Nathan had been standing. Turning, he narrowly avoided a fork coming his way. The man who attacked him was wearing a dark jacket with a hood. Nathan couldn't see his face, but he glimpsed dark eyes gleaming with murderous intent.

His attacker pulled the fork back to strike him a second time. They were not talking, both of them absorbed by the fight.

Suddenly, a loud booming voice exploded in the silence of the barn. "Aha! I've got you surrounded. You can't escape."

Nathan couldn't believe his ears when he heard the voice. He grabbed the knife from the post, trying to avoid using his gun unless absolutely necessary. The attacker threw the fork in his direction without aiming precisely and ran out with Deputy Brett Lockhart in pursuit.

How on earth did Lockhart know where Nathan had gone? Ah, the dispatcher. Nothing was secret in this town, or in the Sheriff's Department.

A shot was fired. Nathan hastened after Lockhart to stop him from shooting everything in sight including the neighbor's cattle.

Lockhart was beyond the boulders, looking down in a very steep canyon. "I winged him for sure. Look at these droplets of blood. But he escaped down into the canyon. I bet he knew a path down there. He knew his way around. We could try to follow him and ..."

"No," Nathan said using his command voice. "We are not going down there without knowing the way or how many they are. This was not one solitary robber. A gang is hiding in these remote parts."

Lockhart was torn between disappointment at not chasing after the attacker and interest in the existence of serious criminals. "Why are they hiding here?"

"We don't know. The sheriff would like to keep it a secret for now, so as not to show our cards until we find out more about their intentions."

"Ah, I see. Mum's the word," Lockhart said with a cutting gesture over his mouth. "But when we discover more, I hope we'll all be involved. In fact, I volunteer to…"

"Not yet. Your help will be very important later. Now please help me carry the old rancher home. He was hit in the head."

Lockhart was still mulling over the facts. "Yeah, sure."

Nathan had one more thing to tell Lockhart. "Thank you for coming to help." Nathan would have preferred to do this alone, but it was the right thing to say. "I know you don't like me because... Why don't you like me?" Nathan asked, curious if Lockhart would admit his own prejudices.

"Because you came with your decorations from the Army..."

"Marines," Nathan corrected him. "I was a Gunnery Sergeant in the Marines for fifteen years of my life."

"You see what I'm saying. You came with your fancy title and all the work we did before didn't matter anymore. You were the hero."

Lockhart was envious of Nathan for the hell he'd been through fighting the enemy in far away countries. Go figure! Lockhart wanted a piece of the action.

"Why didn't you enlist?"

Lockhart looked far away without seeing, lost in thought. "They didn't want me because of a heart murmur some doctor heard. Stupid, I tell you. I've been healthy and strong as a bull all my life."

Nathan understood him better now. All Lockhart

had wanted in life was to fight the enemy. And he was denied this.

"I'm sorry, buddy." Nathan patted his arm in commiseration. "I know you would have made a splendid Gunnery Sergeant."

"Do you really think so?"

"I know so. You'd have been the best."

CHAPTER 9

When he returned home, Nathan saw several boys fighting farther down the street. He knew that Joey must be right there in the middle of the scuffle. The kid had a special talent for finding trouble.

He came closer and indeed Joey was swinging wildly with his right arm, while keeping his left hand protectively over his chest.

"Hey, quiet down," Nathan ordered.

One by one, the older boys stepped back, still circling Joey.

"I know what you said, mister, but he started fighting," one of the boys said, pointing his finger accusingly at Joey.

Nathan looked at Joey. Usually, he would have dismissed the idea as ridiculous. No kid would start a fight with four boys that were bigger than him. But Joey would jump into a fracas without any chance of winning if he felt he was right. "Is that true? Did you start the fighting?"

Looking down, Joey nodded. "Yeah."

"He stole our dog," another boy said.

This time there was no need for confirmation. Joey's shirt shook and a ball of white fur with beady black eyes came out. He had a rope around his neck and his fur was dirty and singed in several places. The tiny animal was still shivering.

Joey kept his hand over him, holding him inside his shirt. "They were dragging him on the ground and burning his fur with a lighter," he explained, wiping his eyes with his hand.

"Is that true?" Nathan asked. "The law does not allow you to torture a human or an animal." In fact, he had no idea if the law cared enough about a tiny puppy in order to mention it specifically, but he thought it was the right thing to say. As a law officer, he should protect animals as well as humans.

"We were training him to run faster," the taller boy explained.

"By burning his fur? I don't think so. Which one of you is the owner of the puppy?" Nathan asked.

"No one, mister. We found him in the street two blocks yonder."

"I see. Look boys, I know it's summer vacation and you have a lot of free time on your hands. Try to do something more useful than terrorizing little boys and animals. If nothing else works, then play some ball. It will be autumn soon and you need to be in good shape when the sports season starts. Now go home and leave Joey alone."

The boys didn't wait to be told twice. They scattered down the street.

Joey smiled at him through his tears.

"And you . You have to be more careful when you pick a fight," Nathan admonished him. "If I hadn't come home right now, those boys would have made mincemeat out of you."

"I know you come home at this hour," Joey replied and threw himself at Nathan, holding the puppy to his chest. "Do you think I can keep the dog if no one wants him?"

Nathan patted him on the back. "I wish I could

say 'yes', but it's your mother's decision. A dog is a lot of responsibility. He needs food, vet visits, daily walks. A young dog has a lot of energy and you have to play with him. You have to clean after him when he has accidents."

"I can do that."

"Then there is Mrs. Taylor. It's her house and, at her age, we can't ask her to take care of a dog too."

Joey looked at him with big blue eyes, just like his mother's. "She'd do that. She had a dog a while back and he became old and died. She loves dogs."

When Laura returned home from the hospital later that evening, the little dog had been cleaned, fed doggy food from TJ's pantry, and was snoring happily in Joey's lap. The idea of separating the boy from the dog and sending the little animal to a shelter was not acceptable. It would break both their hearts. Laura didn't even try. She didn't know how she was going to manage a full time demanding job, a very active boy, and now the extra care of a puppy.

In the evening, after Joey had gone to bed happily with the puppy at his feet, Laura came into the back yard to watch the stars. Nathan was waiting for her in one of the wrought iron lawn chairs.

"Hey, pretty lady, how do you like the new addition to your family?"

"What can I say? He's adorable and he'll be a heap of trouble for me and a lot of extra work. But Joey is happy, so I guess we'll be okay."

"Come here," he said patting his lap. "Let me show you the stars. When I was a kid in Santa Fe, I used to look at the starry sky every night. Do you know that the sky here is one of the most beautiful there is? Because we are at high altitude and the air is clear, not polluted like in big cities." He buried his nose in her soft, flowery smelling curls.

"Yes, it's beautiful here. I'm glad I moved from Colorado Springs. It was time for my brother Joe to live his own life, and not to feel that he needed to take care of me permanently. Maybe I came here thinking that Jack McRavy would take care of me and Joey. Not financially. My nurse's income is very good. But I thought he would protect me from bad people, unpleasant memories, and life's difficult moments."

"It must have been a terrible disappointment for you that Jack married another woman," Nathan said, wondering if she was in love with Jack despite her denials.

"It was in the beginning. I blamed myself for not giving him a chance when he'd wanted to date me. But you know what? I'm happy now. I like my job very much and I have a good income. This is important to me, to be independent. I made friends at work and here. I feel good about myself. I've grown up."

"You certainly did," Nathan whispered, kissing her hair. Would she ever want him if she didn't need him? He was afraid that he didn't have much to offer. His less than whole self, sewn up by the surgeons the best they could, and a career of deputy sheriff in small town, Wyoming. It was true that she loved living here, but he was no bargain. How on earth was he going to convince his beautiful, perfect Laura to marry him?

Unaware of his thoughts, Laura sighed, content to stay safe in Nathan's arms and to admire the stars above. Then she remembered that she wanted to talk to him about an important issue. "Nathan, do you know a rancher called Monroe?"

Nathan frowned. "Yes, I know Monroe. His ranch borders the old Richardson's spread. He has seven sons."

"Seven?" Laura asked.

"Yep. His wife left him and went to live with a sister in Cheyenne. He visits her there sometimes. Why do you ask?"

"I saw a patient today. An adorable toddler. His mother was young, only nineteen years old. She told me her story and it broke my heart. Her father had worked for rancher Monroe several years ago. They had a fight for some obscure reason and Monroe fired him. She admitted that her father used to drink, so it's not clear whose fault it was. At the time, she was in love with Monroe's son. I don't know which one of them. I had no idea they were seven."

Although initially distracted, Nathan quickly

became interested in the story. "I met only three of them. The older two and the youngest. Ethan, the eldest, is married to a woman from Montana, but she left him and he returned home. I don't know much else."

"Yes, well, the story gets more complicated. Because the old men had become enemies, they forbade their children to see each other. However, it was too late. Rachel was already pregnant. When her father found out, he threw her out in the middle of the night. She tried to contact Monroe's son, but his phone was turned off or not working. Not knowing what to do, she went to Denver to stay with her aunt until the baby was born. She was sure the Monroe boy would try to find her, but the months went by and he never came."

"That is quite a story. I wonder which one of the seven is the father of her baby. Wait, I remember that there are twin boys who are in college in Denver."

"It can't be one of the twins. He couldn't be so heartless not to call her if he lived there."

"Unless he had no idea she was in the same city, or maybe he thought she had abandoned him."

Laura covered her eyes with her hands. Nathan hoped she was not crying. She was emotional and easily impressed by the plight of others. "Now she returned back here and her father doesn't want to talk to her. She's renting a studio apartment and works at the middle school cafeteria, where she can bring the boy with her. She is barely surviving. She could use some help and she'd like to tell the boy's father about their son."

"She should be practical. Perhaps the boy's father doesn't know or perhaps he ignores her. It doesn't matter. She should ask for a DNA paternity test and then for child support. He can't ignore a court summons."

"Oh, Nathan, she doesn't want to alienate him."

"Unfortunately, life is hard and she has to do what's best for her baby. If she is afraid of suing him in court, then the next best thing would be to go with the child to the ranch and ask the family if they care about the grandson. You know, Monroe is not a bad man, he loves his children and I bet he'd be ecstatic to see his first grandson."

Laura clapped her hands. "What a wonderful

idea. The little one is charming. I'm sure they'll love him. I hope I can convince Rachel to do just that."

"And I hope you're not going to be disappointed. Life is not always a happily ever after story. It's sad and difficult, and people are stubborn." Nathan stopped talking. No point in scaring Laura. He was not an expert in family affairs. Neither his mother's family, nor his father had wanted him. He was a loner and had lived fifteen years of violence. What did he know about families? He didn't have one.

He didn't realize he'd voiced his thoughts out loud.

Laura cupped his cheek. "You are not alone. You have us. And TJ and yes, even Jack. Families are not always the ones biologically related. Real families are people who love and help each other and stay together through thick and thin."

She gave him the sweetest, most passionate kiss he'd ever dreamt of.

CHAPTER 10

Nathan was driving his patrol cruiser to the Monroe's ranch when he saw a red, sports car stopped on the side of the road. An unusual sight for a country road in Wyoming, mostly because it was an impractical car for driving around here. Not only it was too small and too low for the uneven pavement, but it was convertible. All the dust on the road would blow in the driver's face and hair. He parked his SUV behind it.

The driver's door opened and a young woman stretched out her long, tanned legs first, then climbed out from behind the wheel. She wore a tiny pair of denim shorts and a top, shrunk at a good inch or two above her midriff. She had a pair of high heeled sandals that were suitable for her car, but definitely not for life on a ranch.

Getting out of his car, Nathan shrugged. What did he know about fancy fashion for women? Besides, Miss Sports Car was not his responsibility.

He had just had this thought when he found himself with the woman plastered all over him.

"I'm so glad you saved me, Officer. I'd have been lost here in the middle of nowhere…."

Nathan tried to extricate himself from her hold, although it was not easy. She hung on tenaciously to his shirt. "Ma'am, I'm a deputy sheriff, technically not a police officer. I'm Deputy Nathan Young."

"Nathan," she said, fluttering her long – too long to be real – lashes.

"Hmm, call me Deputy Young. Now, what seems to be the problem here?"

Finally, she let go of him to check if her eyelashes were still on. "I got lost. Without your timely arrival to save me, I'd have been prey to wild animals," she announced dramatically.

"Not so, ma'am. This is a state road. There are not many wild animals here, unless that sneaky bull of Monroe's escaped his pen again. You wouldn't want to face him. Where did you intend to drive?"

"To the Monroe ranch, but my phone lost signal and the GPS was lost with it. Plus I got distracted and did not see that my tank was empty. I'm so glad you saved me," she said and launched herself at Nathan again.

"Whoa," he said, catching her wrist before her arm hooked around his neck again.

"Call me, Ashley. Are you from around here, cowboy?"

"I'm from Santa Fe, New Mexico, but I spent my last fifteen years with the Marines."

"Ah, a brave soldier."

"No, ma'am. As I said, I was a Gunnery Sergeant with the Marines." It was pointless, he thought disgusted, to explain to her that a Marine was not a soldier and should never be called that. "Now hop in the cruiser and I'll take you to the Monroe ranch."

"Wait, what about my car?"

"Don't worry, Monroe will send a ranch hand to pour gas in the tank and bring it to the ranch."

After a long debate about which luggage was more important to be taken in the cruiser, Nathan simply loaded all her luggage in his car and they were off to the ranch.

"Are you a relative of the Monroes?" Nathan

asked in order to make polite conversation and to divert her from her attempts to place her hand on his thigh at every bump in the road.

She wrinkled her nose. "Yeah, you could say that. Are you married, deputy?"

The question took him by surprise. He figured that if Laura claimed they were engaged, he could too. What's good for the goose… and so on. "Almost. I'm committed to the most wonderful woman in the world."

"I'm impressed," she said dryly, looking anything but impressed. "It's always like that in the beginning. Nice words, charming behavior. I was swept off my feet like that, too."

"You're married?" Nathan asked.

"Not for long. I'm going to tell him that this time is truly the end. I'm divorcing him. I thought he loved me. I believed him and all I got was heartache," she said, wiping carefully imaginary tears from the corners of her eyes. "He said I could have anything I want. All I wanted was to experience more in life than what that dusty Montana town had to offer. What do you think he did?

He accepted the first job he was offered right there, as professor of animal husbandry at the college in town. He claimed it was his dream job."

What could Nathan say? "I don't know the situation, but it's clear to me that you two have different goals in life."

"You're right." She sniffed delicately. "That means we should part ways."

"I didn't say that." Since when had he become 'Dear Abby' to give marital advice? Better to steer clear of such situations. "Two people are rarely alike. Most of the time, we have to compromise with the other person in our life."

"But it's unfair. Why should I compromise?"

"I don't know the details and I don't think I should. The only opinion I can offer is to search your heart for answers. If you love, truly love him, then you will want to follow him to the ends of the earth. If not.... then there is no point in talking."

Nathan stopped the car in front of the ranch house, happy not to have to give more advice. Monroe himself came out of the barn, a smile on his face when he saw Nathan. The smile froze and his eyes widened when Ashley climbed down from the truck.

"She's your relative, Monroe. I found her stranded on the state road."

Monroe shook his head in denial. "No, she can't be." He looked around at the ranch hands, who had gathered to enjoy the sight of a pretty woman, grinning like fools. "Where do you think you're going, girl? To a pool party? This is a working ranch. Go cover yourself in decent clothes."

Ashley was not easily intimidated. "You old billy goat, what do you know about being decent? You didn't bother to come to our wedding. You have no right to tell me what to do." She poked him in the chest with her finger.

Nobody had ever dared to talk to Monroe so defiantly. None of his seven sons and certainly none of his hired hands. His eyes bulged and Nathan feared he'd have a stroke. "This is my land and I have the right to tell anyone here what I require of them." He turned to the grinning cowboys. "You have your orders for the day. Go. What are you waiting for?"

"Wait," Nathan said. "One of them needs to go to pick up the girl's car from the road."

The house door opened and the two elder Monroe brothers came out laughing, until Ethan saw the girl. "Ashley," he cried, running down the porch steps to her.

"You know this person, I assume," his father said. "If she is who I think she is, then you'd better take her inside and dress her in proper clothes."

"I want a divorce," Ashley wailed.

"Good idea," Monroe muttered. "Wouldn't Ethan be so lucky?"

"I can't live in a family of barbarians," she continued.

Ethan picked her up in his arms and took her inside, deaf to her protests and complains.

"Welcome to my world," Monroe said opening his arms dramatically. "Not only do I have a big ranch to run, but I have seven boys and not one moment of peace. Let's go to my office, Nathan."

"There is also the matter of Ashley's luggage. All six of them," Nathan reminded him.

"Six? Judging by the way she was dressed, you'd think one small bag would suffice."

Monroe's office was not in the house. It was a small room off the tack room in the barn. With so many kids, every room in the house was needed. Despite the small size, the office was cozy, with a pot-bellied stove in a corner, an old scarred wooden desk, and two comfortable weathered leather chairs. There was no fire in the stove now because it was summer, but it was useful in winter.

"Coffee?" Monroe asked, bringing in a fresh pot from the coffee machine.

"Yes, thank you."

"The doctor said it's a bad habit, but who can survive an entire work day without coffee?"

"Do you have heart problems?" Nathan asked.

"A murmur and a valve problem, but who has time to care about that? As long as I'm alive, I'm busy and I don't have time to pay attention to this. I take my pills daily. It's enough." He sipped the hot coffee, and smacked his lips appreciatively. "Now, tell me what brings you here? I assume it's not just to bring that impertinent girl."

"No. Ethan did that on his own entirely. I came to talk about several issues. First, the fires at midnight are set by intruders and they are not rustlers. If someone is still stealing your cattle, then that's a different person than the ones lighting the fires."

"You're right. No cattle were missing recently."

Nathan took a sip of coffee and continued. "I have a link, but I'm not sure it's connected to your intruder. Last month, a gang of bikers terrorized the ranches around Laramie. They destroyed Myrna Richardson's vegetable garden and when the rancher forced them away with his rifle, they threatened to come back. They returned and set fire to the side of the house."

"Oh, yes. I heard about that. It happened just last month, before Iris married the sheriff and the Richardsons moved to town."

"We caught two of them, but the leader escaped. Now I heard that he is back in town searching for something. My informant didn't know what he was looking for. He may be the one lighting fires at midnight on your land." Nathan sighed. "Also, someone attacked Richardson a few days ago when he went to check on his vacant old house. That intruder vanished somewhere in the canyon, behind the boulders, near the house. It's all tied to the cursed canyon, but what could they be looking for there or on your land on the other side of the canyon?"

Monroe shrugged. "I can't think of anything. There is no oil here and even if it were oil, the land is mine and so are the mineral rights."

"No, they are not looking for oil. It would be something smaller and easier to remove."

"Beats me. I don't know. Unless the fools are looking for Lamont's hidden treasure."

CHAPTER 11

"What is Lamont's treasure?"

Monroe coughed in his coffee. "It's a legend. That's what it is. Nothing more. Jimmy Lamont was a famous gunslinger and stagecoach robber from the 1870s. Later on, he used to rob trains and even banks. He worked alone and didn't trust anyone. Maybe that's why he was not caught for a long time."

"Interesting."

"Yes, it is. Maitland knows more details. He is writing a book about the history of this corner of Wyoming."

"Was he caught?"

Monroe nodded. "The railroad company placed a high reward on his head, dead or alive. A bounty hunter caught up with him and Lamont was killed in the fight. To everyone's surprise, he had no money or treasure of any kind with him when he was killed. Or so the bounty hunter claimed."

"Nothing was recovered?"

"Not one cent. It was naturally assumed that he'd buried the treasure, but this is a vast land. Where do you start searching? As I said, the robber, unlike others like him, had no known family or even a sweetheart. He liked to gamble. It was assumed that he lost most of the money, but he never paid with jewelry or even the gold nuggets that he acquired robbing a mining company in Colorado."

Nathan smiled. "People started searching for his treasure. I understand. But why here?"

"Because he was hunted from Colorado to here and he knew it was only a matter of time before he'd have to confront his pursuers. It was assumed that he had hidden his treasure first, hoping that he'd come back to it later."

"But he was killed instead."

"Yes, life was precarious in those times no matter on which side of the law you were. In fact, sides were not clearly defined. Many people who started a life of crime, later turned around to become lawmen. The reverse is also true. Righteous, respectable men succumbed to temptation and ended up as criminals. But to answer your question, the story says that Lamont was caught in these parts, north of Laramie. It was assumed he buried his treasure somewhere around here."

"Interesting as this is, it is only a story."

"Of course. But children and grown-ups alike enjoyed talking about it and imagining what fun it would be to recover Lamont's treasure. So much so, that at some birthday' parties, we liked to organize a treasure hunt, with clues all over the place."

"I see how kids might have fun hunting for treasures, but it's improbable that our night fires are lit by people looking for a supposedly hidden treasure."

"Improbable," Monroe agreed. "But I've seen adults doing a lot of improbable, silly things. It's not impossible for a crazy man to think he's close to digging out a fortune."

"All right. This case is like a mirage. The closer I think I am to solving it, the more complicated it becomes. I'll see what I can do."

"Is there anything else you want to talk about?"

Nathan set his empty coffee mug on the desk and rose to leave. "I promise you I'll catch whoever made those fires and attacked Richardson." He placed his Stetson on his head, but there was another issue nagging him. "Tell me, did you have a fight a few years ago with one of your hands and had to fire him?"

Monroe laughed. "I've had a lot of employees that I had to fire over the years. Most cowboys work here only temporarily. They hire for the season, then leave to take part in rodeo competitions or hire somewhere else. Most of them are reliable and do their work, but there are also many who are not."

"This guy used to drink and had a daughter in high school. I don't know more about him, not even his name. His daughter's name was Rachel."

He saw instantly a flicker of recognition in the older man's eyes before they shuttered. "Is he in trouble with the law? Is that's why you're asking?"

"No. Not that I know of," Nathan admitted, realizing that he needed to come clean if he wanted Monroe to answer his questions. He hesitated. It was not his truth to tell and the first one to find out about the baby should be the presumptive father. In the past, he wouldn't have given this mess a second thought. It was not his problem. Did he feel a new kind of responsibility for the people in this county since he had become their deputy?

Right or wrong he had to try. "This girl is in a difficult situation. I'm asking you not as a lawman, but as a friend. I consider you a good, reasonable man. Which one of your sons was her boyfriend around two years ago?"

Monroe got up from his chair and looked Nathan in the eyes. "Why?"

"That's the problem. I think the boy should know about her. That she is back in town."

"They were together only for a few months."

"Jeez, sometimes one night is all it takes, not a few months."

"Give me her address and I promise you that I'll help her."

Nathan shook his head. "You'll bully her and

frighten her to leave town. I respect you, Monroe, but you are very autocratic."

"And you, at almost half my age, are not intimidated by me."

Nathan rolled his eyes. "After what I went through in Iraq and Afghanistan, nothing can intimidate me. I'll text you that address. I trust you to do the right thing."

Nathan saluted and left. Outside, the ranch hands had brought the sports car and parked it in front of the house. Now they were circling it in wonder. It looked like a toy compared to the big trucks parked there.

"Shoo!" Ashley shouted at them from the porch, dressed in a summer dress. It was not much of an improvement to the shorts she'd had on before. The dress was nice, but rather sheer and when a wind gust blew… well, you'd wished she was wearing the shorts.

The men instantly transferred their attention from the car to the pretty girl on the porch. Yep, Monroe had a big problem on his hands – Nathan thought driving away.

When a day starts on the wrong foot, it's a sure thing that it's not going to get any better. Nathan parked his cruiser in front of the Sheriff's Department and made his way to his office. What he saw there froze him on the spot in the doorway.

Near the window, Laura was seated in a chair, like a queen. His shy emotional Laura was laughing loudly at a joke that Deputy Lockhart told her. She was entirely absorbed in a cozy chat with his nemesis. Lockhart looked like a besotted fool, grinning with his mouth stretched from ear to ear.

Nathan had never felt anything akin to jealousy in his life, but right now he felt ready to tear Lockhart apart. "Laura," he said sharply.

"Ah, Nathan, I'm glad you finally showed up. Brett here was so nice to keep me company and he assured me you'd return soon." Laura looked at Lockhart smiling. The idiotic deputy preened like a peacock under her praise. "I need to talk to you," she said and her smile faltered unsure of his dark mood.

Jack was not in the office today, and that was a

more private place to talk. Nathan grabbed her hand and pulled her after him, ignoring Lockhart's protests.

"Now, see here, Deputy, I don't like your caveman behavior," she said, sitting in one of the chairs in front of Jack's desk.

His Laura had come a long way from the scared mouse she'd been before. Nathan smiled at the thought, until he remembered her friendly chat with Lockhart. "Deputy Lockhart is not someone you should associate with."

"He was nice and polite with me, unlike others I know…" She looked at him from under her long lashes.

"Let's agree to disagree. Now, tell me why you came here. I assume nothing wrong happened since you were having such a fun time with Lockhart."

Laura fumbled with her purse and looked at him again, trying to gauge his mood. "I had a break and I wanted to talk with you. I know you said you wanted to take Joey to Jack's house to meet his son. You told me and I agreed with it. Now, I found out from Joey, entirely by chance, that you also want to take him to the Gorman ranch."

"You object to the Gormans? They are a respectable family."

"No, I don't object to them. Why should I? But I don't want my son to be placed in a dangerous situation, like riding wild horses." She raised her chin in the air pugnaciously.

Nathan leaned on the desk in front of her and crossed his arms over his chest. "Laura, this is ranch country. Children are taught to ride at a young age. Little Elliott Maitland was placed on a horse by his father when he was two years old."

"I've seen Little Elliott last Christmas. My son is not like him. Joey is small for his age. He inherited his short stature from me. He is delicate and frail."

She hadn't seen her delicate son taking on four bigger boys and fighting with all his might. "Laura, I understand that you are worried for him. Don't be. I was small for my age until I reached fourteen. Afterward, I grew like a beanstalk. You have to let him be a normal boy, play with children his age, and do what the others are doing. Otherwise, he'll be shunned by them and he'll be resentful. I know you are protective and I admire you for that, but there are limits and you have to let him fly."

Laura's lower lip started to tremble, a sign of deep emotion. Nathan hoped she was not going to start crying. He'd never intended to upset her so.

"You don't know that. You don't know how it feels to be a parent. Joey is not your son. How could you feel…?"

Nathan stiffened. He was not a parent, but it hurt that Laura thought he didn't care for Joey because he was not his father. "Do you think I can't love Joey because I'm not his biological father? Do you think his own father loved him more?"

"No, I … I don't. I think that you took over our life and decided what is best for Joey on your own. I think that perhaps it would be better to cool things off."

Nathan closed his eyes. It was not easy to be rejected. Laura hadn't promised him forever, but he'd hoped. How stupid of him. He turned to the window and looked outside. Outside, it was a sunny summer day, beautiful and warm, but in his heart, a storm raged. He could fight and try to explain, but what chances did he have of convincing her? If she felt pressured or cornered, then she'd be deaf to all his arguments.

She may be right. He had no experience at being a parent. He loved Joey as if he were his own, but love was not enough. He could have been wrong in his decisions concerning the boy. Maybe he had steamrolled them and Laura knew better what was best for her son. It was clear that this implied their relationship had to cool off too. Without including Joey, it went nowhere and it had no future.

"Very well. I had no right to interfere. I'll step back."

"You will?" she asked, unable to believe he'd given up so easily.

"If that is what you want, then yes, Laura. I see now that I bulldozed my way into your life and it made you uncomfortable. I never wanted that. I thought you felt the same and I wanted to help. I'm sorry," he said still in front of the window, looking outside. He was afraid that if he looked at her, he'd break down and would be unable to say what needed to be said.

Laura came near him. "I have to do what is best for Joey." She touched his arm, asking him to understand.

Nathan stepped to the side, away from her touch. Maybe he was defective in some way that no one ever wanted him. He remembered how as a kid his dad sent him to visit his Native Americans relatives in Oklahoma, his mother's family. He'd been so excited to meet them and find love and acceptance there. But they rejected him. 'You're not one of us,' they said over and over, until he finally understood that they were not his family either. Where was his place in the world? He'd thought that Laura, Joey, and he could be a family together. Not so.

"Rest assured I'm not going to interfere in your life again. Good bye, Laura."

CHAPTER 12

You'd think he'd had enough for a day. But no, the day was not over yet. He parked his car in the driveway as usual. Joey was nowhere in sight. Not that he was looking for him. Laura had made it abundantly clear that his interference in their life was not welcome.

Of course, it would be difficult to continue living here, next door to her. He needed to find other lodgings. Or perhaps better yet, he should talk to Jack and resign and go to Oregon as he'd planned in the first place. There was nothing for him there either, but it was just the same wherever he went. Oregon it was – a man had to have a plan.

He went inside to talk to TJ. He found him at his desk, working at his computer, looking from time to time at a plate filled with muffins from Cora's bakery.

Despite his unhappy state of mind, Nathan couldn't stop himself from laughing. "What are you doing, exercising your power of restraint?"

"This is my reward for when I'll finish my work,"

TJ said looking at him over the rim of his glasses. "What about you? That hangdog face says woman trouble."

Nathan took a seat in one of the comfortable chairs near TJ's desk, stretched his long legs in front of him, and snatched one of the flavorful muffins from the plate.

"Hey!" TJ protested. "Don't you know it's not healthy to drown your sorrow in food? Tell me what happened."

"Laura decided that she doesn't want me in her life and that I don't know what's best for Joey. That I don't care about him."

"And what brought this about?"

"I wanted to take him to Jack's house to meet his son and the Gorman boys, so that he could learn to ride with them. She thought it was too dangerous for Joey." Nathan rubbed his eyes. He had not felt so tired in ages. "She might be right. What do I know about raising a child?"

"More than she does, I'm sure. She got scared and tried to put some distance between the two of you.

That's what she did with Jack. She lost Jack and she'd probably lose you. Except that this time, she ignored that Joey already considers you a father figure and he's not going to accept the separation."

"You think so?"

"Mark my words. She'll be back, crying with her beautiful blue eyes, sobbing on your shoulder. I don't think she's worth the trouble. But if you want her, you'll get her. She'll be back."

They were interrupted by the doorbell ringing. Nathan went to answer the door. He had a premonition before opening the door. It had been such an unusual day. What were the chances it would end the same way?

Not even his maternal grandfather, who claimed to be a shaman and clairvoyant, could have guessed who was the middle aged man in front of the door. Nathan had the shock of his life.

It'd been fifteen years since they'd seen each other. His father was thinner and older. His smile was not as cocky and self-absorbed as before. It was wavering, as if he was uncertain of his reception. Strange. His father had never been uncertain.

"Hello, Nathan," he said simply, as if they'd parted yesterday.

Stepping aside, Nathan let him in. "What are you doing here?"

"I heard you were discharged from the army and I came to see how you're doing." His father stopped in front of TJ. "I'm Simon Young, not so young," he joked extending his hand.

"TJ Lomax. I'm Nathan's roommate."

"TJ is in fact my landlord. But you probably know that since you found me here. I didn't give you my address."

"I'll leave you two to talk. I'm going to heat up some lasagna for dinner and make coffee." TJ said diplomatically, going to the kitchen.

Nathan looked after him, then back at his father. "I'll ask again. Why are you here?"

The same hesitant smile. "I heard you were wounded, then discharged, and I wanted to see how you are doing."

Nathan shook his head. "Nope. You didn't care how I was doing for fifteen long years. I don't think you were struck by curiosity right now. Besides, I was wounded more than a year ago and the Marines let you know. You did not care then to find out if I lived or died."

His father looked down at his hands. "I had some difficulties then…."

"Right. Your paintings were not making a grand splash in the artistic world in New York City."

If Nathan expected a sarcastic reply, he didn't get it. His father just smiled sadly and shook his head. "There comes an age when a man needs to get his affairs in order."

"Cut to the chase, old man. If you need money, then you are barking up the wrong tree. A Marine is hardly a rich man."

"I didn't come to ask for money. I came to see how you're doing. I know it's hard for you to believe, but this is the truth. I know I haven't been the most dedicated father…"

"To say the least," Nathan scoffed.

"It was what it was. I didn't come here to apologize for what can't be changed."

"I don't expect apologies, but you should also not expect me to open my arms and say, 'Daddy, you finally came. You remembered you had a son and came.' Because it's not going to happen."

"Why are you so resentful, Nathan? I thought you enlisted because you wanted more freedom. You got it."

"I enlisted because I had no choice. There was no money for me to go to college. And I got involved in a silly prank. As usual, I had to face the judge alone. You couldn't be bothered to help me. Enlisting let me off the hook with the judge and offered me the chance to get a degree while serving in the military."

They were interrupted by TJ who came to call them to dinner. "You can sleep here. Next to the office, there is an alcove with a couch," TJ said to Nathan's father.

"Not necessary. He won't be staying." The same moment Nathan answered, his father smiled to TJ.

"Thank you. That's generous of you. I accept."

There was not much else to say during dinner, except enjoy TJ's lasagna. After that, Nathan left them to play chess and debate politics. He went outside in the back yard. He intended to look at the stars, not at the house next door trying to guess which window was Laura's and if she was asleep or perhaps thinking of him and having second thoughts about rejecting him.

A scratching noise near the fence put him on alert. Was the little dog outside investigating the bushes in the back yard? One of the boards was carefully set aside and Joey's small body squeezed through.

"You shouldn't be out at night without telling your mother," Nathan observed. Joey froze near the fence when he heard his voice in the dark. Nathan continued, "Maybe she is right after all. I am a bad influence on you."

Joey ran to him and climbed into his lap. "No, you're not. Mama said I can't go to meet the other boys and to go riding. Why not?"

Nathan patted his back. He was thin and small for

his age, but he was not delicate and frail. There was a wiry quality to his thinness, doubled by a daring and stubborn character. No, Joey was not a mealy mouthed mama's boy afraid of facing life's hurdles straight on. "Didn't your mother tell you why?"

"She said I'm too small to go riding with them." His voice trembled.

Nathan did not have any experience being a father, but he felt Laura didn't explain this right to the boy. Certainly, this was not going to improve Joey's confidence. "I don't want to contradict your mother, but I don't think you are too small. The boys who grew up on these ranches learned to ride when they were smaller than you. Your mother loves you and wants to protect you. She is afraid for you. That's why she preferred to keep you safe and not risk an accident."

"But you don't think I'm too small to meet the boys and to ride?" Joey persisted with his questioning.

"No, I don't think so. But my opinion doesn't matter. Your mother is the only one who has the right to decide what is best for you. She honestly believes this is the best."

Joey leaned against Nathan and kept quiet for a while. Then Nathan heard his voice hesitating to say out loud his next thought. "Mama said that you are not going to visit with us in the future. Is it because you're mad at me for not going to meet those boys?"

"This is what your mother said?"

"No. She didn't explain this."

"Let me tell you something, Joey. No matter what, I care very much about you and your mother. This feeling can't be switched on and off. I will always care." Nathan took a deep breath. "Your mother felt that the two of you are better off living alone, without my daily presence and constant interference in your life. I can't blame her. After what she's been through, it is understandable that she is afraid to trust the wrong man and to repeat the mistakes she made in the past. She is responsible for you, so she needs to be twice as cautious. She decided this is safer for the two of you. I have to abide by her wishes."

"I want you to be my father," Joey said in a

barely audible voice, his face buried in Nathan's shirt.

Nathan felt his heart was breaking. "Oh, Joey. I want this too, but I don't see how this can work if your mother is afraid to trust me. Who knows? Maybe she's right. I don't know much about being a father and my entire life was one war or another. Maybe she's right not to trust me."

Joey placed his small hand on his cheek. "I trust you."

Nathan felt like laughing and crying in the same time. "All right. Time to go to bed. Perhaps tomorrow will be a better day. Let's get you safely on the other side of the fence."

While Nathan led little Joey to the fence separating the two properties, a window downstairs closed silently and the old man smiled to himself. What do you know? He almost had a grandson. Of course, young people didn't know that life is short and unpredictable and they shouldn't waste time. A little push in the right direction might help.

CHAPTER 13

Nathan opened the top drawer of his chest looking for a clean shirt. There was a brief knock on the door and his father entered the bedroom.

Nathan turned, surprised. His father's polite smiling face changed into a horrified look. Nathan grabbed the first shirt on top and placed it in front of his naked torso. But it was too late. His father had already seen the damage the war wounds had done to his body.

"Oh, Nate, I'm so sorry." His father had never called him Nate, not even when he was a little boy. The fact that he did now showed how deeply shocked he was.

"Not pretty, eh? What did you think war was? A walk in the park?" Nathan turned back to finish dressing.

"I never thought it was. I'm very happy that you returned alive. I want you to know that I have always waited for news from you. I'm glad that at least you let me know that you were alive. I prayed for your safety every day. I am proud and I respect you for how you lived your life, for your service to our country."

Slowly, he stepped out and closed the door behind him, leaving Nathan looking surprised after him. His father must be getting maudlin in his old days. He'd never cared. Why now?

But then a new question consumed him. If his father was horrified by Nathan's scars, how would a delicate woman like Laura feel? The idea of undressing and have sex in the dark didn't appeal to him. He was only thirty-two and he wanted to have a woman to love him and to have a family. Was he so hideous that no woman could look at him without turning away? Then, what was left for him?

The Sheriff Department was humming with the usual morning noise. Nathan caught up with the sheriff on the hallway.

"Jack, do you have a minute?"

"Sure. Come in my office."

Jack took a seat behind his desk and looked with satisfaction at a box with two blueberry muffins from Cora's bakery and a steaming mug filled with fresh coffee. "Help yourself to a muffin. They are out of this world delicious," Jack invited Nathan.

"No, thank you. I had my coffee earlier and TJ made the mistake of allowing my father to prepare breakfast. His greasy omelet stuck to my stomach."

"Sorry to hear that," Jack commented, biting with relish into the flavorful muffin. "Your father came to visit?"

"Yeah. After fifteen years, he finally remembered he had a son. But that is not what I wanted to talk to you about. First, I want to thank you again for agreeing to invite Laura's son to meet Garrett and the Gorman boys. Unfortunately, it's not going to happen. Laura decided that Joey is too small to ride, so I'll have to cancel the whole plan. I'm sorry, Jack."

"Nonsense. You said he's six or seven years old. That's just the right age to learn to ride and Tom Gorman is a very careful rancher. His boys ride adequate horses, smaller, mild-tempered and…"

"I know, Jack. You don't have to convince me. Laura panicked. She asked me to back off from their life because I've taken over and she needs to be in control. Or something like that."

Jack's half-eaten muffin remained suspended mid-air to his mouth. "You mean, that silly woman got scared again and chased you away? She rejected you like she did with me."

"You know, she's not crazy. After what she's been through, it's natural to be more cautious and not trust the first man that smiles her way."

Jack set his empty coffee mug on his desk with a clank. "You are not the first and neither was I. I understand that she's cautious, but in this case it borders on the irrational. She is not only hurting good men, but also her son. He will start to feel alienated and avoided by other kids because he is not allowed to play with them. Is he as mousy as his mother?" Jack asked frowning. If Joey was a scared rabbit, then there was no way his fearless son could be friends with him, even if Laura allowed it.

Nathan smiled. "He is small for his age, but what he doesn't have in stature, he makes up with his daring character. I found him fighting four bigger boys who had ganged up on him."

"Well then, more's the pity. I'll talk to Laura."

"No, Jack, please don't. I don't want her to feel pressured to do anything."

But the sheriff's mind was made up. He made an evasive gesture with his hand that meant neither yes, nor no. "Tell me what else you know about the mysterious fires at midnight on Monroe's ranch."

"They are camp fires for some people who are looking for something."

"On Monroe's land?"

"Apparently, yes. They are close to the canyon that separates Monroe's land from Richardson's property."

"Hmm, that's not where the rustlers' tracks were. And why at night?"

Nathan shrugged. "I don't know. I assume that if they were searching or digging there for a long time they couldn't do it during the day because Monroe's men would see them. Not to mention if what they are doing is secret...."

"Or illegal."

"On the other hand, I found out that Coyote is back in town and I don't know if this has anything to do with the fires."

"What? I'll arrest him for arson charges."

"Not yet. If he is involved with the fires, then we'd better discover the whole story first. He is searching for something - I don't know what – and he has a map. A map on paper. I assume it's an older map."

"A map of the Monroe ranch?"

"A map to lead them to whatever they are searching for. I haven't been able to connect all the dots from Coyote's search to the midnight fires. But Monroe told me an old legend about a bandit who lived one hundred fifty years ago and who supposedly buried his treasure in these parts, right before the bounty hunter caught up with him."

"Oh, not about the famous Lamont treasure. Old Man Maitland told me about it. That's only a children's bedtime story. There's nothing real to it," Jack scoffed.

Nathan raised his hand. "I'm not saying it is real. However, crazy people like Coyote, who believe in getting rich without working, might think it's true. Especially if they have an old map to lead them to the buried treasure."

Jack rubbed his eyes. "I see. There are all sorts of loony people out there who make our life more difficult. All right, Nathan. I'll let you connect the dots, as you said."

Later that day, the sheriff drove to the hospital. The receptionist jumped from her chair when she saw him. "Sheriff, I hope you weren't wounded again?"

"No, my dear. I'm perfectly all right. I didn't know people in this county cared that much about my safety," he said joking.

"Yes, sir. We care very much about the safety of our sheriff." She leaned forward. "Many young women wept into their pillows when you married the Richardson girl."

Jack's jaw dropped. He'd never imagined that the

women in this county dreamed about him at night. He had to tell Iris, so they could laugh together.

The receptionist looked at him questioningly, and he said, "I need to talk to one of the nurses in pediatrics, Laura Delaney."

"Ah, pretty Laura." Jack raised one eyebrow, so the receptionist hastened to add, "Of course, business is business."

"Just so. I'll wait here in this waiting room. If she's busy, please let me know, and I'll come later."

Just five minutes later, the elevator doors opened and a worried looking Laura came into the waiting room. Jack signaled her to join him in a more secluded corner of the room, where they could talk in relative privacy.

"Jack, what happened? Is it Joey?"

"No, Laura, nothing happened to him. Relax."

"Nathan. Is he hurt?"

Now that was interesting. "Would you care if he were hurt?"

"Of course I care," Laura snapped.

"The way I heard it, you told him to keep his

distance from you and your son," Jack said still smiling, although his eyes were hard and unyielding.

She looked away from him. "He was taking over our life."

"He wanted to help you and especially your son, to ease his way making friends with boys his age now during summer vacation. In the fall, when school starts, he's not going to feel awkward among his classmates. What's wrong with that?"

"You don't understand," she cried. Then she looked around and toned down her voice. "Joey is small for his age and not so strong. He's a fragile boy. He's not able to keep pace with stronger boys. Nathan had no right to interfere."

Jack's eyes narrowed. "The fragile boy was fighting four boys bigger than him in the street."

"What? No."

"Laura, you can't keep him isolated from the world. All you can do is prepare him for life and support him. Otherwise, he will chafe under your restrictions and run away. I know because I have a son of about the same

140

age."

Laura waved her hand. "But he's not exactly your son."

Jack kept his composure with difficulty. Laura stepped back, realizing she'd upset him. When he spoke, every word was said distinctly. "Garrett is my son legally and in every way that matters. He and Iris are my life. No biological father could love his son more than I love him." He considered abandoning this mission. It had been a mistake to try to reach Laura, but there was one more thing to be said. "You hurt a wonderful man, who didn't deserve to be treated this way, a hero, who almost gave his life fighting overseas, a man who has suffered a lot and who wanted to help. I understand your fears and I warned him about you. But what you don't understand is that you also hurt your own child. The boy needs a father figure, a man to look up to, and he couldn't find a better man than Nathan. You rejected him, but your boy is not going to accept your decision."

Laura's blue eyes filled with tears. Jack placed his Stetson on his head with impatience. A man in white coat approached them.

"Any problem here, Laura?"

Jack turned and looked at the man. 'Dr. Jones' was written on the pocket of his white coat. The doctor recognized the Sheriff and nodded. "Sheriff."

"No. No problem. We're done. She's all yours, buddy," and saying this, Jack patted the other man's arm, almost making him lose his balance. Then he left, winking at the receptionist, who blushed and waved back at him.

CHAPTER 14

Back in his office, Nathan looked morosely at mug shots of Coyote. Every time he was arrested, he had a different alias and a different ID. This was not an easy case to crack. Maybe he should let the sheriff arrest him. They had plenty of evidence that he was the arsonist who tried to destroy Richardson's ranch house.

Deputy Lockhart came in the office whistling and his cheerfulness grated on Nathan's nerves. "Do you have to be so chirpy in the morning?"

Lockhart didn't seem fazed by Nathan's bad mood. "Wake up. It's past noon, if you want to know. I nabbed a petty thief who tried to get away with a six pack of beer from the liquor store. He was underage, so he avoided facing the store attendant and paying for the beer."

"Weren't you ever a teenager doing stupid things, eager to impress your peers?"

Lockhart looked at him like he'd just landed from the moon. "Sure, I was. But I never agreed to do anything illegal. Respecting the law is important, otherwise we'd have chaos."

That answered Nathan's question. Lockhart would never have painted the principal's house in rainbow colors and think it was fun.

Lockhart had other things on his mind. He continued to look out the window. "Say Young, you promised to let me know about the intruder at Richardson's ranch. I hope you don't intend to leave me out of the action."

"I haven't learned anything new. I'll keep you posted."

"And how is our little lady?"

It took a while for Nathan to understand what Lockhart was referring to. And when he did, a cold fury took hold of him and he clenched his fists. "If you're talking about Laura, and for your sake I hope you're not, there is no 'our lady'. She's mine," he said in a deadly tone. It was not exactly true, considering that Laura had rejected him, but he was not going to let Lockhart know this news.

Lockhart was not easily cowered. "Contrary to what you think, Young, I don't fear you, decorated war hero that you are. I would pursue the lady because she is the most beautiful woman I have ever met. She is also good, soft-spoken, and attractive in a gentle, feminine way, not aggressively sexy like the actresses splashed on the tabloids."

Surprised that Lockhart had such insight, Nathan nodded. "True. She is special."

"She is perfect. She is the ideal I've dreamed of my entire life. I don't fear you. I would pursue her regardless of your warning. There is only one thing that stops me. She looks at me with friendship and not much interest, but she looks at you like the sun rises with you. Why would she do so? Darn if I understand."

"Hmm," was Nathan's answer.

Lockhart continued his musings. "I could never understand women. They don't seem to like me much. It's not like I'm ugly. I cut quite a dashing figure in my uniform."

"You need a wife. Why don't you go to the

Cowgirl Yarn shop?"

"Are you making fun of me, Young? Because if you are, I'm not amused."

"I'm not making fun. There is a circle of knitting ladies there, known to be the best matchmakers in town. You could go there and say you need a gift for your great-aunt Euphemia. You don't need to say much else. The ladies will take over."

"I'd feel like the proverbial elephant in the china store. Besides, this is Laramie. Everyone knows me since I was in shorts. They know there is no great-aunt Euphemia."

Nathan set aside the mug shots on his desk. "Maybe that's the problem. They've known you since you were a kid and don't consider you seriously. You could go and say you are investigating a crime and want to ask them if they saw a prowler or thief or any other suspicious activity."

Lockhart gave him a dubious look. "What serious robber would want to attack the yarn shop?"

"True. The old ladies are rather scary."

Lockhart looked at him for a long time.

"What?" Nathan barked, unnerved by his stare.

"I'll visit the yarn shop, if you'll go with me to a shooting range."

Nathan wouldn't have been more surprised if Lockhart had asked him to chase aliens in deep space. "For fifteen long years, I fought in one war or another. Trust me I had enough shooting to last me a lifetime."

"Come on, are you afraid I'll best you? We'll have a competition, the fastest and best shooter from three rounds. What do you say?"

Nathan shook his head. "You are crazy, man. You can't beat me. I am professionally trained. I'm a Marine."

Lockhart narrowed his eyes. "Do you want to bet?"

Nathan leaned back in his chair and crossed his arms. "What do you want? If this is about Laura…"

"No. It's not. This is about us. Like two gunslingers from the past. To see which one is better. It's not a duel. It's a competition." As he spoke, Lockhart became more excited about this idea. "The prize will be the fame of being the best."

It had been over a month without a drop of rain, Nathan thought, looking at the dried grass and bushes along the road to Monroe's ranch. It was July and many of the locals were attracted by the Cheyenne Frontier Days and the rodeo competition. The younger ones competed in the rodeo. The ranchers supplied the livestock for the events.

Maybe Joey would enjoy going to Cheyenne for the week-end to watch some bronc riding or steer wrestling. Then he remembered that Laura had warned him to stay away from them. No doubt she'd consider rodeo events too rough for the boy.

But Joey would be thrilled to watch the competition and to be there among the cowboys. Nathan just knew that his eyes would sparkle with excitement. For the boy's sake, it was worth trying to convince his mother, even with the risk of provoking her ire.

At the ranch, he landed in the middle of a

domestic scene. Ethan was standing in front of the house looking at one of the upstairs widows. The cowboys were standing in a circle at a distance watching with interest what was going on.

"…in this godforsaken corner of the world." Ashley's voice resounded through the open window and an embroidered pillow flew out right in the middle of the circle.

The men cheered.

"I bet the next one will hit Ethan right in his noggin," a shorter one said, twirling his moustache.

The next projectile to fly out the window was not so soft. It was a large piece of pottery with flowers in it. "…And you can take your measly bouquet with you." Ethan was lucky to jump from the spot right before the vase shattered in tiny fragments. It was an ugly vase of a bilious green color, but still… for the effort the maker had put into creating it, perhaps it could have found a better use.

"…you think I'll sacrifice my youth…" A bunch of – were those underwear? – flew out the window and landed all over the broken pottery.

The men cheered.

"…and my beauty…" What followed were socks, definitely socks.

Cheers again.

"…you are mistaken." Ashley stuck her head out the window, waved at the men who were cheering her, looked around for Ethan and volleyed a bunch of t-shirts at his head.

"What is going on here?" The cowboys parted to let John Monroe come closer. He dismounted and signaled to a younger cowboy to take care of his horse.

"Ashley threw a hissy-fit because I told her I like spending the summer on the ranch and in the fall I'll return to Montana to teach," Ethan explained.

"Aargh!…" Another pillow flew through the window landing at Monroe's feet.

The rancher looked at it disgusted. "Son, were you blind and deaf when you married that shrew?"

A tall cowboy slapped his neighbor on the back. "He-he, maybe deaf, but definitely not blind." The other one elbowed him in the ribs. "What? She is easy on the eyes."

Ashley came to the window again. "I heard you old man. I'm a shrew, am I?" And the third pillow landed squarely on the rancher's chest.

"She does have good aim," commented the mustachioed ranch hand.

"Ethan, pick up your underwear from the yard and make that shrew shut up." Monroe turned around. "You don't have any work today? Am I paying you to do nothing?"

The men went back to work. The show was over, at least for the moment.

Looking at them from under his bushy eyebrows, Monroe signaled Nathan to follow him in his office.

"Tell me, Deputy, what should I do? I have become the laughingstock of my men," Monroe complained, collapsing in the chair behind his desk.

"Nothing. It's not your problem, but Ethan's. The way I see it, as long as he is looking to you to fix his marriage, it's not going to happen. Ethan needs to act like an adult and face his own problems. If he thinks he can change his wife and they can compromise, then it's all good. If not, then both of them have to decide to separate."

"That would be a pity. I don't believe in divorce. What happened with vows of forever, I ask you? "

"I wouldn't know, sir. I've never been married. But sometimes there are indeed differences that can't be overlooked. In such cases, divorce is better than a miserable life together," Nathan said thinking of Laura's first marriage.

"Too bad. With that fiery temper of hers, she'd give me strong grandchildren. I love Ethan. He's my firstborn son. However, he is soft spoken like his mother. He is not weak, but he prefers to back away from confrontations. I'm not happy, but I have to admit that being a college professor suits him better than being a rancher."

What could Nathan say? It was not his business, but Monroe needed to talk to someone. "You're lucky to have seven sons. I don't know the younger ones, but look no farther than Connor. He loves this land and he is a good rancher."

"Hmm. Connor is not perfect either. By the way, did you bring me that girl's address?"

"I did. Monroe, if you go there and try to bully her to leave town, I'll be very upset. I respect you, but you don't want to mess with me. I've fought bigger and trickier enemies than you."

"You're half my age, Deputy. Don't threaten me. We had a deal and I promised to set it right, didn't I? I have plenty of enemies myself. My land yonder, near the canyon, looks like a lunar landscape. Blacken stones of fire pits everywhere. There is nightly activity of some sort, but what?"

Nathan poured himself more coffee from the pot nearby. "They are searching and possibly digging. Let me see what else I can find today and I'll return tomorrow to spy on them."

CHAPTER 15

It was late in the evening. The sun was setting, but there was still light. It was warm and balmy. A gentle breeze was rustling the tree leaves from time to time. Mrs. Taylor's old rose was filling the air with a subtle perfume.

Laura had brought a cushion for the stone bench, and her Kindle. She closed her eyes lazily. This was the best time of the day, after her work was done and when it was too early to go to bed. A couple of hours to enjoy and relax.

Joey was inside with Mrs. Taylor and a nice older gentleman playing pinochle. Laura declined to join them and went in the back yard instead. She had a very interesting new mystery book, but she couldn't get into the story. Snippets of the conversation she'd had earlier that day with the sheriff, kept intruding and diverting her attention from the storyline.

What if the sheriff was right and she was not a good mother for Joey? And what of Nathan? Had she been wrong to tell him to stay away from them? She missed him very much. He was the only man who knew how to talk to her, to be gentle and compassionate, and to give her self-confidence. He had a calming effect on her, alleviating her fears. In his presence, it was like her world righted itself.

She knew Nathan was a good man. Joey was already attached to him. And yet, when he'd come closer to them, all these reasons disappeared and she pushed him away, scared. Was she meant to live alone, fending off the attention of men like Dr. Jones? The sheriff's scorn hurt, and she had to admit that she missed and needed Nathan.

She watched spellbound as two boards from the old rotted fence were set aside and the man of her dreams tried to push himself through the gap. His shoulders were too wide and he didn't fit, not even sideways.

"Wait." Laura left her Kindle on the bench and ran to the fence. It was so rotten that she pulled another board and set it aside with little effort. "Mrs. Taylor will evict us for damaging her property and we'll be homeless," she said trying to keep her voice serious and not to smile widely. Her eyes were bright and sparkling.

"I'll fix it later," he said, feasting his eyes on her. Just like that, he forgot everything he'd come to discuss. He caught her waist and brought her closer. She didn't pull away. She never had before either. Strange how she accepted his physical presence, yet rejected the idea of his interference in their lives.

Then all reasonable thought melted away as he kissed her with all the pent-up desire he felt for her. Laura answered like she wanted him with the same intensity.

The fence squeaked and Nathan stepped away from it, continuing to hold Laura in his arms. "We're going to bring this entire fence down if we lean into it," Nathan whispered.

Laura giggled. The image was hilarious. She leaned back to see him better. With her index finger, she smoothed the fatigue lines at the corner of his eyes.

"I came to tell you that I won't accept your order to get out of your life. I can't," he said simply. "I promise

I'm not going to push my way against your will and contradict you."

"Then what are you going to do?"

He grinned. "I'll try to convince you." He pulled her to him again, watching for her reaction, and kissed her slowly.

"Like this?" she asked breathless.

"In any way that I can." He honestly hoped to convince her that they were meant to be together because he couldn't let her go.

"Is that why you sneaked in, demolishing Mrs. Taylor's fence?"

"I wanted to talk to you. This month, The Frontier Days and Rodeo competition are taking place in Cheyenne. I think Joey would enjoy this. I want to take both of you there this week-end."

"Nathan,…"

"I'm asking your permission first, Laura, as you can see."

Laura touched his face. "I trust you, Nathan. I'm still afraid, but I'm willing to have an open mind."

"You'll see Joey will like it."

"That's what I'm afraid of. That he will like it so much, he'll want to try it too."

With a mighty squeak, a good part of the fence between two posts, collapsed behind them. Nathan pulled Laura to the side and turned his back to the fence to protect her

The light on the back porch was turned on and from the doorway Mrs. Taylor asked, "What happened?"

Before Nathan could explain, his father came on the porch near Mrs. Taylor. "Well son, you don't have to destroy the fence in your haste to reach your lady. You could have used the side gate. It is unlocked."

Nathan was so surprised to see his father there that his jaw dropped. Squeezing between the two adults, Joey ran down the porch straight into Nathan's arms.

"I'm so happy to see you. We played this great game of cards, you'd have liked it," Joey said. Thinking his father had taught Joey poker, Nathan's heart had a hiccup at the idea. He wouldn't put it past the old geezer. "Pinochle," Joey filled him in. Nathan breathed easier.

"Don't worry, Mrs. Taylor, I'll fix the fence tomorrow. Better yet, I'll call some guys working in construction and you'll have a brand new fence in no time at all."

Mrs. Taylor waved her hand. "The fence was old and rotten. There is no rush. What's the point? Leave the fence with this gap until you two young people reach an understanding. It will make life easier."

"How very true, my dear," Nathan's father said, and after depositing a kiss on her wrinkled hand in European style, he walked down the porch stairs into the yard. "Since the fence is down, I guess this is the shortest way. We might as well take it. Good night, my dear Lydia," he said. Then he winked at the old lady, who giggled like a teenager, and he disappeared on the other side of the broken fence.

"That was my father." That was all Nathan could think of saying. Frankly, he was too stunned to make sense.

"Really? You didn't tell me he was so charming." Laura looked thoughtfully after the older man.

"I didn't know he was. I haven't seen him in fifteen years."

Next day, in the afternoon, Nathan finished his work later than usual. There had been a fire drill at one of the department stores and he had to assist together with representatives from the Fire Department.

Now he walked down the hallway of the Sheriff's Department to the exit. He had to go home quickly to change from his uniform into jeans and a t-shirt and drive to Kate's diner for his weekly meatloaf with mashed potatoes and hopefully to meet with Good Old Bill.

"Excuse me," someone called after him.

Impatient, Nathan turned. "Yes." The words died in his throat. The man calling him was about the same age as him, tall and well-built. An eye patch covered his left eye and a jagged scar crossed his cheek. Despite the slight limp, his posture was straight and Nathan knew immediately this was a military man like himself.

"You're a Marine," Nathan said, guessing.

The man opened his mouth to rebuff him, like

Nathan did when a civilian asked an intrusive question or was too curious about military details. Something in Nathan's stance and the inflexion in his voice, made the man more relaxed. He recognized a brother in arms. "Navy SEAL."

"Ah. Welcome home." They shook hands, nodding in perfect understanding of what the other had been through.

"Could you point me to the Sheriff's office?" the man asked.

"Sure. This way. You might be lucky to find our sheriff here. As a newly married man, he likes to go home without delay when his work is done." Nathan led the way to Jack's office. "If not, then perhaps I could help you with whatever issue you have. I'm Deputy Nathan Young, formerly Gunnery Sergeant in the Marines."

A lopsided smile transformed the somber Navy SEAL into a very attractive man despite his scars. "I knew you were a Marine. Dane McRavy is my name."

Nathan stopped to look at him. "Are you related

to our sheriff?"

"Yeah. I'm his brother." He said without the usual happiness of seeing a brother you missed. Nathan knew that long years on the battleground in foreign countries, followed by brief time off, could lead to estrangement between members of a family. If you added to this the fact that while the family continued to live in about the same way as before, the military man went through events that changed him forever, then communication becomes difficult, if not impossible.

He knocked on the door and opened it to see Jack at his desk. "Jack, you have a visitor," he announced and stepped aside to let the Navy SEAL enter.

Jack raised his eyes and froze. "Dane," he whispered, white-faced like he'd seen a ghost.

Maybe that's what they all were for their families, ghosts, and returning home was nothing short of a miracle – Nathan thought. Luckily for him, he didn't have a big family. He doubted his father had lost much sleep wondering if Nathan would return, despite of his claims to the contrary.

Nathan turned to leave the sheriff and his brother reunite in privacy. He was ready to close the door behind him, when he heard Jack call after him. "Nathan, please stay."

That was a strange request. Why would Jack need Nathan's presence in a personal family discussion? But this was not the moment to ask questions. If Jack asked, then he must have his reasons. Nathan came back in and took a seat in one of the two chairs in front of Jack's desk.

Jack signaled his brother to sit in the other chair. There was no jumping of joy, hugging, back-slapping, laughs and cries, as one could expect of such reunions. It was more like they were assessing each other like two future combatants in a ring.

CHAPTER 16

The sheriff looked at the papers on his desk without really seeing. "When you left I thought it was a mistake and you'd come back. You left without warning, without saying Good-bye. You left me with mom and dad and with a ranch that should have been yours."

"I was a silly kid of seventeen," the Navy SEAL said.

Looking at him now, it was hard to imagine him ever being a silly kid.

"I was seventeen also when I enlisted," Nathan popped into the conversation. Jack looked at him like he didn't know what he was talking about, while Dane kept the same impassive face and ignored the remark. Nathan's understanding and sympathy were all for the military man, but Jack was his friend. He'd do his best to diffuse the obvious tension between the two brothers.

"I was a kid too and you left me alone and confused, with two parents, for whom the sun stopped shining when you left," Jack continued.

164

"I know," Dane agreed. "In retrospect, I understand now. At the time, I was battling demons of my own and they were overwhelming."

"Pshaw! Because Lucinda left you…"

"Lucy didn't exactly leave me," Dane corrected softly. "She was shown the door."

Jack opened his mouth, then snapped it shut. Finally, he asked, "Our mother …?"

Dane nodded. "Our mother told her that I was too young to know my own mind. I wanted to marry Lucy and go to college to get a degree in agricultural studies. Eventually, I'd have returned home to the ranch."

"Why didn't you do just that?" Nathan asked.

"Yeah, why didn't you?" Jack said.

"To make a long story short, I didn't know the truth. It was one of those unbelievable, idiotic stories of misunderstanding and miscommunication. Mom told me Lucy came to say she's leaving town and me because I was not good enough for her, and I believed Mom."

Nathan went to the coffeemaker and poured freshly brewed coffee in three cups. They all needed it.

Dane accepted the coffee gratefully. He waved his hand. "It's all water under the bridge. Why are we talking about this old story now?"

"Because it's unfinished business and we need to know what happened to create this rift between us," Jack suggested rubbing his eyes. "How did you find out the truth about Lucy?"

"She sent me a letter, several years later, through Dad. It found me six months after it was sent. She alluded at how Mom had chased her away. She was married, happily I assume, and expecting her second child," Dane explained, sipping the hot liquid from time to time.

"Hmm, was it difficult out there in the war?" Stupid question, but how else could he bridge the gap of all the years apart? Jack didn't know how to approach this stranger who looked vaguely like his brother, but was completely different.

"I don't talk about the war. Ever. At all. You can ask the Gunnery Sergeant here. He'll tell you the same. War is not like memories from a camping trip. Most of it is classified information anyway."

"We are two strangers, Dane. I need to find my brother," Jack tried to explain what he felt.

"If you think you'll find the naïve young boy who used to dream under the big tree in our back yard, then you're going to be disappointed," Dane warned him.

"I know… I'm still hoping to reconnect with my brother, my partner in adventures, in pranks, in shared dreams. I'm glad you came to find me. I have many questions. How long is your leave?"

Dane looked at him. "Forever. My days in the military are over. As you can see, I'm not able to be a Navy SEAL any longer. I've been discharged."

"Do you regret it?" Jack asked with curiosity.

"Of course, I do. The military career was all I had and all I knew how to do. Being discharged makes me feel useless, like a horse retired to pasture before his time."

Another lost soul like himself, Nathan thought. He had been lucky that the sheriff had almost forced him to accept being a deputy. It gave him a purpose in life and it brought Laura and Joey into his life.

"You never wrote to me, Dane. Not once in recent years."

"Most of the time I couldn't. Then, I didn't know where you were. Mom said you left Texas and didn't leave an address or even an email address."

"So how come you're here? How did you find me?"

"Dad told me. I googled you as soon as I was discharged. Imagine my surprise to find you sheriff here. Last I heard, you were with Dallas Police Department."

Nathan looked at his watch and rose. "I have to go, Jack." To his surprise, Dane got up too, grabbing the edge of the desk for balance.

"Wait, I'm coming with you."

Jack looked at his brother confused. "Why are you going with Nathan? Aren't you coming home with me? You have to meet my wife and son."

"I have to find a place to eat and one to sleep, in this order." When Jack opened his mouth to protest, Dane raised his hand to stop him. "You married recently.

You don't need a houseguest to intrude on your privacy. Jack, give us time to get to know each other again."

"Are you more comfortable with Nathan?" Jack asked, feeling slightly hurt.

"I don't plan to be his houseguest. He is a Marine and understands me, even if we don't swap stories from the battlefield. There is an unspoken kinship. I am more comfortable with him than any other. Sorry, Jack. I intend to visit you and meet your wife. I didn't know you had a son. That is news."

"I adopted him last month. But I couldn't love him more if he were my own biologically."

The brothers hesitated before awkwardly hugging each other. Then, Nathan left accompanied by Dane. Nathan matched his steps to Dane's slower gait.

"You know, Jack is a wonderful person. I don't want to interfere, but he would be happy to have you live with them."

"Not yet. I'll be here indefinitely. There's nowhere else I need to be. There is time." They stopped near Nathan's cruiser. "If you can point me to a place to eat, I'd be grateful," Dane said.

Nathan turned to face him. "I can't invite you to lodge with me. My father came unexpectedly and he is sleeping on the couch. My landlord invited him. We are already very cramped. However, if you follow me home to change my clothes, then we'll go to a place where you'll eat the best homecooked meal since you enlisted."

Dane considered this, and then accepted. "Thank you."

On their way to Kate's diner, Dane talked about his brother. "I'm glad that Jack got married. I hope he's happy."

"Yes, he is. Iris is a wonderful girl."

"Iris. Hmm, interesting name. I can picture her, beautiful, soft-spoken, agreeing with Jack in everything."

Nathan chortled amused. "You couldn't be more wrong, my friend. Iris Richardson is a tall, strong woman, beautiful in her own way. She is a veterinarian doctor, very good and competent. Jack adores her and she loves him, but she's not shy. She tells him her opinion, even if she disagrees with him. They are happy together."

"Strange. I always thought Jack would marry a woman very different than our mother. She can be overbearing sometimes, and she thinks she knows best."

"Iris is not overbearing. She's a career woman, independent, who tells it as it is. Nothing wrong with that. She loves Jack and she's not ashamed to tell him this often."

Nathan stopped the truck in the parking lot at Kate's Diner. Dane got out and looked around.

"Are you sure this is the right place? I mean I've been in much worse places, but I was hoping for a quiet, nice dinner, without having to turn at the slightest noise and check for my gun."

"This is a truck stop. It can get rowdy at times, but don't worry, Kate is able to quiet down the worst of her customers. Her food is delicious."

Nathan opened the door and entered. Dane followed. In the beginning, their presence didn't attract attention, but little by little the noise died down, the customers stopped talking, and all eyes turned to the newcomers. Some of them knew Nathan, but Dane's tall, imposing figure, his scars, and eyepatch drew attention. So much so that Nathan wondered if indeed he made a mistake bringing him here.

The unusual silence in the room attracted Kate from the kitchen. She wiped her hands on her apron and looked around the room. She focused on Dane and raised her eyebrow questioning at Nathan.

"Hi Kate, I brought a friend for dinner. I hope your meatloaf is ready for us."

Kate nodded. "It sure is. You and your friend are welcome. Take a seat and Hannah will bring it to you immediately." She looked around at the staring customers and one by one they turned back to their food and conversation.

Nathan saw the old carpenter at a table in the back and made his way there. "Hi. This is my friend, Dane."

The older man smiled. "I'm Good Old Bill. Please sit down. I thought you were not coming today.

This is my second helping of coconut pie," he pointed to the plate in front of him.

The server, a tiny slip of a girl, brought their steaming plates. Carefully she set them down in front of each one of them. It was obvious she was not accustomed to waitressing.

"Where is Hannah?" Nathan asked.

The girl worried her lower lip, not sure if to answer. "Hannah had an accident in the kitchen. I'm Minnie. I'm only a helper. I wash dishes."

What could Nathan say? That Minnie was too young to work in a place like this? It was not his business.

"Hey, girl," a burly trucker shouted from two tables down the row. "Bring us more of that hot sauce. Come now, you hear?"

The girl stumbled and Dane caught her hand to steady her. Then he turned and stared at the trucker. "She'll come when she's not busy."

The trucker went back to his food and the girl whispered, "Thank you," and ran back into the kitchen.

CHAPTER 17

Good Old Bill set down his fork and sighed with satisfaction. "Good pie. Almost as good as my Edna's. And that says a lot. Kate is a good cook."

Both Nathan and Dane were busy shoveling the succulent meatloaf with creamy mashed potatoes into their mouths.

"This is tasty," Dane said, between two bites, when he sipped his cold lemonade.

"I told you so," Nathan said, continuing to eat.

Good Old Bill looked from one to the other. "You served together in the military," he concluded.

"Not together, but we both enlisted and served wherever was necessary," Nathan answered. "You can talk freely. Have you found out anything new?"

"Not much. Coyote is expecting a man to deliver him a better or newer tool. An instrument to do… whatever he is doing. This will happen in a couple of days. He plans to try again after that, at night, to find what he is searching for. I'm sorry I couldn't discover more details."

Nathan patted his hand. "You did well. It occurred to me that instead of going there at night trying to catch him in the act, I should go there tomorrow during the day to investigate."

"Can I come with you?" Dane asked, although he had no idea what Nathan was looking for. "I don't have anything else to do, except for finding a place to live."

Good Old Bill studied him with interest. "Are you out of the military like him?"

"Yes, I've been honorably discharged. Now I have to figure out what to do in a civilian life."

"What would you like to do?"

The question took Dane by surprise. He had not thought beyond connecting with his brother and readapting to regular life. "I was born on a ranch. I thought that would be my life. The ranch was sold, so I don't have a place to return to. I could buy land here, to raise horses, no cattle. I'm good at fixing cars. I always had this dream of restoring old cars to their previous glory. Other than that, I have a military pension that is adequate."

Good Old Bill beamed at him. "Good, good. You see, you have a plan and I have an idea. My house is not big and I live alone, just me and Belinda, since my poor Edna passed away. I've been… uneasy since Coyote moved next door. You could move in with me until you find a better, more permanent place. You could hear better than me what they are talking about behind the fence and we could prevent who knows what crime."

Dane was stunned by this unexpected offer from a man he'd just met. He had no idea who this Coyote was and what he was supposed to hear. He presumed it was okay if Nathan knew the man. "But if you live with this Belinda…"

"What? You don't like chickens? Some of them can be aggressive and peck at your hand when you try to remove the eggs, but not my Belinda. She's as gentle as a lamb. Clo, clo, clo, she talks to me."

"Belinda is his chick. I mean a real, live chicken," Nathan explained, barely containing his laughter.

"She is the only one left in the coop to keep me

company. Now, are you going to live with me or not? I don't think you big Marines fear a dainty chicken."

"Navy SEAL. I was a Navy SEAL. Thank you for your generosity. I accept."

They paid the bill and were ready to go. Dane had to go first with Nathan to his home to get his truck, which he'd left there.

"Pst, pst!" They heard from behind the dinner. Dane turned and the helper, Minnie, came running to him. She rose on her tiptoes and kissed his scared cheek. Then she pressed a small coin in his palm. "It's my lucky penny. I want you to have it." And then she ran back to the diner.

It was late at night when Nathan finally had time to go in the back yard, knowing that at this hour Laura was in bed, yet hoping that perhaps she was not. There she was, stepping carefully over the fallen section of the fence and looking for him through the greenery.

"Hey, pretty lady, are you searching for me?" he whispered, smiling in the dark. "Come here and tell me how your day was." He lifted her up ignoring the complaints from his torn abdominal muscles and set her on his lap. He buried his nose in her honey blond hair. Mmm, it had the sweet flowery smell that he'd become addicted to.

"Not bad. A child suspected of dangerous meningitis, was feeling better today, and the blood tests came back negative. And you were right; Joey was ecstatic when he heard we're going to Cheyenne to see the rodeo competition Saturday."

"It's more than rodeo. There are Wild West reenactments, a museum, an Indian Village, a Grand Parade, and carnival rides. It's going to be spectacular. The entire town comes alive. It's fun."

She leaned against him. "I met Dr. Jones today in the cafeteria. He's a pest." She shook her head, biting her lower lip.

"What is it? Did he bother you, Laura? I can have a talk with him and I guarantee that he'll never say another word to you after that. In fact, he'll try his best to go the other way when you cross paths in the street or in the hospital."

Her soft, caressing palm cupped his cheek. "I appreciate it. But it's not necessary. You see, I realized that I don't fear him. And trust me, there are older, experienced nurses who shake in their boots when they see him He's a terror to work with. Shouting during surgeries, throwing instruments on the floor."

"He should be fired."

"No. It's not possible. He is a genius in his specialty. There is no other like him. Although Dr. Kovacek is good too, and nice. About Dr. Jones, I don't mind having to reject him. I was just wondering if I should perhaps wear a ring to be more convincing."

Nathan hid his laughter in her hair. "Absolutely. Are you asking me to marry you?" he joked.

"What? No, no. This is serious. Marriage is a chain…" She breathed heavily and clenched his hand with a force he'd never suspected she had. "No, no."

She was having a panic attack. Nathan cursed himself and his loose tongue. "Laura, look at me, sweetheart. It's me, Nathan. I could never hurt you.

Never. If you don't want to get married, then we don't have to. Not now, not ever. I will be here for you as long as you need me. No marriage, no chain. Only love. Let me love you, Laura. Relax. Like this. Look at me and breathe deeply. Like this. Again. Are you better?"

"Yes, thank you. I might never get over this unreasonable fear. It is too deeply rooted inside me. Like a defense mechanism. One day, you'll decide that I'm not worth the trouble and you'll leave me, like Jack did," she said with sadness.

"No, I'll never leave you. I can't live without you. I'll always be here."

"Give me time, Nathan. In my mind, I know you are a good man. But marriage sounds permanent and unchangeable, like a prison. It's scary," her voice trembled and her eyes were glittering with unshed tears.

"It's all right. I'm not going to lie. I want to marry you so that the entire world will know you're mine and so that I can protect you better. I would like to have children. But I accept your decision."

She sighed looking up at him. "At the shelter, we

had a professional therapist. She was good, and told us all the right and encouraging words. But deep down, this fear beyond reason is still there. Sometimes at night, I jump awake with my heart racing. Not from nightmares. Just like a warning – don't sleep, beware of danger. Crazy, huh?"

If he could get a hold of her ex-husband, Nathan thought he would tear him apart. What kind of monster could abuse and frighten a gentle, sweet soul like Laura?

He didn't realize he'd voiced this thought out loud, until he heard her answer. "The kind that is hidden under the charming face of a handsome man that a naïve woman believes and marries. It was only after a year and a half that he revealed his true self. Now do you understand why I don't dare trust any man? I trust you, but the idea of marriage makes me panic."

"I understand. I really do. People don't understand PTSD, but I do. When I was in therapy, I saw the family of a soldier telling him to snap out of it because he was safe at home and he had no reason to be stressed. Like all the horror he'd been through could be erased in the blink of an eye. So, yes, I understand. I'll be here for you whenever you need me."

The door squeaked when Nathan came in later that night after he'd led Laura back to Mrs. Taylor's house. A small lamp had been left on in the living room. For him? Who could have been so thoughtful?

"Well son, you'll have a long battle ahead of you to conquer your lady's heart, a fight against her fears. But my bet is on you. You'll win." He heard his father's voice from the cavernous darkness of the alcove, where he was sleeping on the couch.

Nathan wanted to snap at him, but he was tired and mentally exhausted. "What do you know about conquering any woman's heart?" His father was self-centered and Nathan doubted he could be bothered to think of another person besides himself.

"Ah, the way to your mother's heart was a difficult one. She was so beautiful, it touched my artist's soul. I painted her every day. Hundreds of paintings."

"I don't remember even one painting of her in our

house when I was a kid."

"No. I put them all in storage after she died. I couldn't bear to look at them. It was too painful."

"Did you love her that much?"

"She was all that was good and beautiful in my life. When she died, a part of me died with her. All that remained was anger at her leaving me and the anguish of living without her. Powerful emotions. It was a lot to paint on the canvas."

Nathan remembered the hideous images that had scared him when he'd looked at his father's paintings in childhood. Did he miss Nathan's mother and was he angry that she died too young and left him alone?

His father continued talking, lost in memories of a time long gone. "It was not easy to win her heart. Not with her entire family being set against her marrying one not of their own."

Nathan dropped in a chair near his father's couch. "They didn't want me," he said, memories flooding him too. He remembered the kid he was then, confused and hurt at his mother's family rejection. "The summer you sent me there. They told me I was not one of them and I was not wanted."

His father answered after a long silence. "I know. At the time, I hoped that they loved your mother as much as I loved her, and that they would accept you as a part of her. Also for you, it was important to know the other half of your heritage. A rich, spiritual heritage you should be proud of."

"In the end, they didn't want me," Nathan repeated.

"It is more complicated than that, Nathan. After losing her, they hurt just as much as I did and they blamed me for her death. I encourage you to try to reach them again. You have cousins and young relatives, who don't remember those times when your mother married me, and if they do, they won't be mired in old resentments and grudges. If they reject you again, then so be it. You have your family now, with Laura and Joey. They are your family no matter how confused Laura is."

In the solitary nights spent on foreign soil, Nathan had often thought of who would be sorry if he never returned and wondered if his Native American family in Oklahoma would accept him now after all these years. "Rejection hurts, no matter how or when."

"I know, son. I hope that, as neglectful father as I was, I never made you feel unwanted. Because you never were. And I'm proud of the man you have become and of what you did with your life. I needed to say this." He turned in his bed sheets on the narrow couch. "Now I have to go to sleep. Good night."

CHAPTER 18

It was another beautiful summer day in Wyoming. A few puffy white clouds adorned the brilliant, blue sky. Nathan and Dane were driving to the Monroe ranch.

"Beautiful country," Dane said, watching the surrounding landscape from the passenger's seat. He had on a pair of dark sunglasses that made him look less piratical than the eyepatch, but equally fearsome. "Different than Texas where I grew up, but beautiful. It's good to be home."

"Amen, brother. I agree with you." Nathan adjusted his own sunglasses against the bright sun glare. He had informed Dane briefly about the strange fires that sprouted at midnight in a remote part of Monroe's ranch. "This land is no more than half an hour drive from town, yet very isolated. No wonder some yahoos are doing unlawful activities here at night."

"On Monroe's land?" Dane asked.

"Well, yes. Technically it's his land. Previously it

was part of Richardson's ranch. Iris' grandparents owned the land. They grew older. Iris was in Denver at Veterinary School. They needed money to pay tuition and they were not able to work as before, so little by little they sold parcels of land and their cattle to Monroe, who was only happy to acquire more land. Behind Richardson's old house, there is a deep and narrow canyon, at one time part of the property. Now, I think it's the boundary between the two ranches."

"And the fires?"

"The fires were seen along Monroe's side of the canyon. But Richardson's house is empty. They moved to town to be near Iris and Jack and a medical facility, should they need it. The last time Richardson went to check on his house, he was attacked and left unconscious. It's a fair assumption that unlawful business is taking place on both sides of the canyon."

"For sure. The clue is in the canyon."

"I want to explore the area in daylight and perhaps we'll find a clue, as you said."

"Hmm. So what happened with Richardson's old

house? Is he going to sell it too?"

"Yes. I assume he will. He's moved out permanently. It's not going to be easy for him to sell it. There is not much land left. Not enough to raise cattle. And the location is too isolated."

"How much land was left with the house?"

"Maybe a hundred acres, maybe less. As I said, not enough to feed a good size herd. I loved the house. It has an old west charm. I thought about buying it myself. I need a house if I'm going to stay here."

Dane looked at him through his dark glasses. "Are you?"

After a brief pause, Nathan nodded. "I think I will. I like being a deputy sheriff and my intended, Laura Delaney, is a nurse at the hospital. Of course, she is not yet convinced to be my intended, but I keeping working hard on this. Anyhow, that's another story for another time."

"What about the Richardson house? Do you want to buy it?"

"I thought about it. But with both Laura and I

having jobs in Laramie, I don't think it makes sense to buy such a remote place. Winters can be rather brutal here. We have to be at work every day. When the blizzard strikes, the ranchers stay holed up inside. Both Laura and I need to go to work. Driving can be treacherous. After a long consideration, I decided that no matter how much I like it, Richardson's property won't suit me."

"Maybe you could show it to me after we finish the investigation on the Monroe's ranch."

"Sure," Nathan stole a glance at the inscrutable Navy SEAL near him. "Are you planning to settle here?"

"I don't have any plans whatsoever. I'm still mourning the abrupt loss of my military career. It happened overnight and I'm trying to come to terms with it."

"Then why do you want to see Richardson's house?"

Dane shrugged. "Perhaps I'm hoping the place will call to me and give me a hint of what I should do."

"I know the feeling. I was asking myself what to

do with the rest of my life, when your brother offered me the deputy job. Jack is a good man."

Monroe's ranch house came into view and Nathan parked near the barn. Loud cries could be heard inside and Ashley burst out like a rider on a wild horse from the chute.

"Ethuuan, I'm going to tan your sorry hide." Ashley was trying to control the horse that was bucking under her like a bronc in a rodeo competition.

Monroe came out of his office. "Who put the girl on that wild horse? Wait. That is a very docile mare. What did you do to her?" he addressed the grinning cowboys.

"Nothing, Boss. She insisted on riding in those high heels. Then she dug them into the mare's ribs. Who can blame her? The mare, I mean," a tall cowboy explained.

"Where is Ethan?"

"In the house. Writing a dis-ser-ta-tion or something like that."

"Go get the horse and make the girl dismount

without any more tricks. Understood?" Monroe looked at his men, who nodded and went to catch the bucking horse. Then he turned to Nathan, shaking his head. "Can you believe it? My firstborn son prefers to keep his nose in dusty books instead of working outside on the range."

Nathan laughed. "No two human beings are alike. My father is an artist, a painter, but it was clear ever since I was a child that I have no artistic talent whatsoever."

"Yeah. I see what you mean. Make no mistake about it, I'm proud of him for being a college professor, but I expected him to inherit my love for the land."

"He did, but in a different way that suits him better."

Monroe nodded. "Deputy, did you find anything new?"

"Not much. But I'd like to see the canyon in daylight if you don't mind. This is Dane McRavy."

"A relative to our sheriff?" Monroe shook hands with Dane, appraising him with interest.

"Dane is his brother. A former Navy SEAL."

"It's an honor to meet you."

Connor approached them and saluted Nathan. "Do you want the cattle moved from the eastern pasture, Dad?"

"Connor, bring horses and ride with them to the canyon near the Richardson land. Zeke will move the cattle. And tell Jeb to fix the fence while you're there," Monroe ordered.

Connor brought horses and they were off riding. Nathan saw that Dane was an expert rider, certainly better than him. Dane was enjoying riding very much. Nathan guessed that it was the first time Dane had gotten on a horse in a long time.

Connor was surly and upset, riding in silence.

"What's bugging you, Connor? Did we mess up your plans for the day?" Nathan asked.

"Not my plans for the day, no. For my life, yes."

That was such an unexpected answer that Nathan looked at him open-mouthed. "What did I do?"

"You told Dad about Rachel and gave him her address."

"So? She barely makes ends meet and her son needs a father." Nathan looked at Dane who was riding in silence, enjoying the day and not interested in the conversation. But Nathan knew that the Navy SEAL noticed every detail. They were trained this way. Finally, he understood. "You're the father."

After a short pause, Conner said, "Possibly I don't know. It was a couple of years ago and she caught me when I had some difficulties deciding what way to choose in life. I was fighting with my old man all the time. Ethan had left home and if I wanted the ranch I'd have to put up with the old man for many long years to come. It was either that or leave and start from scratch."

"Did you love Rachel?"

"No. Not then, not now. She was clingy and assuming, making plans for the future without bothering to find out if I felt the same."

"The way I heard the story was that she and one of the Monroe boys, she didn't say which one, were like Romeo and Juliet. Their fathers were enemies and were against their love."

"Duh, do I look like Romeo to you?" Connor scoffed. "I'm a down-to-earth rancher, not a youthful dreamer. Rachel fantasizes about things that are not real. I never told her that I love her."

"What about the toddler? Is he yours?"

Connor looked at the horizon, before nodding. "I think so, yes Rachel was not the kind of woman who sleeps around. Dad wants DNA testing to be sure."

The lawman in Nathan had to remind Connor. "If he is your son, then you have to take responsibility, and I believe you are a man of honor. And Connor, I didn't create this situation, you did."

"You're right, but I'm upset. The old man went to see her and saw the boy also. That was all it took. He was like under a spell. His first grandson has to live on the ranch, he said. And I have to marry Rachel as soon as possible to provide a father for his first grandson."

Nathan laughed. "It's a natural reaction. I'd say you already are the father of the boy. I heard the boy is smart and adorable. He is a charmer. No wonder Monroe was enchanted. Go to see him. Every little boy deserves a father. And mark my words, if the biological father is absent, the boy will pick another as role model. You don't want that."

"I'll take care of the boy. I don't shirk my responsibilities, contrary to what you say, but the idea of tying myself to Rachel for life is not acceptable. We'll both be unhappy and I doubt it would be good for the boy."

"You're right. Just do what you feel is right."

"I don't know what is right. Dad threatened to disinherit me if I don't marry Rachel."

"Ah, now I see your problem. I'll try to talk to him. It might be only an empty threat. Ethan is not a rancher and the twins have gone to college. Who is Monroe going to rely on, if not you?"

Connor shook his head. "You don't know Dad. He's stubborn. You can't change his mind when he digs in his heels."

"We'll see. Now, enough talking. Let's check the rim of the canyon."

CHAPTER 19

They counted six different blackened circles where fire had been lit. They were at various distances along the rim of the canyon, in the rocks nearby. Some of them showed traces of camping, like an abandoned hurricane lantern, a rusted coffeepot, and a pair of gloves.

Nothing to give them a better idea about the nature of the activities.

"Why did they need so many fires?" Dane wondered, caught up in their investigation. "Were they signaling?"

"Don't start. Dad is half convinced they are aliens." Connor laughed.

Nathan picked up the lantern. "You'd think aliens would have better technology than a propane lantern from Wal-Mart. Besides, farther down that way, you'll find tire tracks."

"Maybe they are regular people camping here."

"Camping on our land? This is not part of the

tourist trails."

Nathan went closer to the rim of the canyon to look down. It was steep and narrow. Connor hunkered down near him.

"They are doing something at night, and they don't want any witnesses nearby. The ranch hands are a superstitious bunch. They believe in cursed places, especially if they are creepy like this crack in the surface of the earth. Cowboys fear ghosts. They believe this place is haunted and, with these fires at midnight, they won't come close to this place, not even in daylight. It is possible the fires were for this purpose, to scare other people away from here."

Nathan made up his mind. "That's it. I'm going down to the bottom of the canyon."

"You can't. There is no way down, no path," Connor told him.

"Every surface can be climbed or descended, with the right equipment," Dane commented. Probably he'd done that numerous times in his dangerous career.

"What do you think we need?"

"For rock climbing, we need ropes, nuts and bolts, carabiners, helmet, harness…"

"Stop right there. We don't have any of these."

"We have rope," Connor corrected him.

"We do?"

"Of course we do. I'm a cowboy. I always have good rope with me."

Nathan cheered up. "Okay. We have rope. The canyon walls are steep, but not like rock climbing. I have to try."

Dane shook his head in disapproval, but Nathan had decided to get to the bottom of the canyon to end this mystery.

They knotted one end of the rope around his waist and looped the other around a rock and knotted into Connor's saddle in such a way that Connor could control the rope.

Nathan let himself slide over the rim of the canyon. At first, he thought it was easy. Connor released the rope little by little and his descent was smooth. There were also protruding rocks and wiry plants deeply rooted in the canyon walls that he could grab or rest his feet on them. Piece of cake.

Then his foot slipped and the rope tightened. At the top, Connor was taken by surprise and for a moment the rope slipped through his hands. Dane grabbed it too and they stopped it together.

Nathan checked it. The rope held. He hoped that if it was good enough for cattle, then it would hold his weight without breaking.

He was almost at the bottom of the canyon, when he grabbed the corner of a rock to his right. To his surprise it gave way. "Wait!" he cried to the ones at the top.

A big hole remained where the rock had been. He pulled a root from the soil and it gave way more until he could see inside. It looked like a cave. He pulled out his flashlight and looked inside. It was a large opening and the ceiling was propped up with wooden beams. Ah, so it was man-made, not a cave. If it was a cave, then it had been enlarged by people.

His curiosity was piqued and he shouted to the

ones at the top. "There is a cave here. I'm going in."

"Not enough rope," Connor answered. "Let me bring another length and knot them together."

But Nathan was impatient. "I'm going in, just to see what's there." He squeezed himself through the opening and looked around. It was dug into the canyon wall and supported by beams and posts. It was old. Maybe this is what Coyote and his men were searching for, but they had not found it. It looked untouched for over one hundred years.

Nathan had a frisson of apprehension. To be the first to find a construction from the past… It was not Native American. He'd seen many houses in New Mexico carved into the rock on the mesas. This was not it.

The opening continued inside the mountain. It was low. Nathan had to walk stooped, but he was not claustrophobic. Narrow spaces didn't make him sick. He went farther inside until the rope tied at his waist stopped him. He untied the knot and left the rope there. Not wise, his conscience told him.

He rotated the beam of his flashlight around him. The person who'd carved inside the rock had had no modern equipment. It had been done by hand with a pickaxe and shovel.

And then he knew what this was. It was one of the many abandoned mines, where a miner had tried to find a mineral ore in secret. Did he find it? Was this mine and its promises of riches what had attracted Coyote here with an old map?

Eager to discover more, Nathan went farther.

He reached a place where the tunnel split. Left or right? He went left, but after a while the tunnel narrowed until it stopped entirely. There were signs that someone had dug in there, but he could not see any distinct vein of mineral. Just plain rocks with flakes of mica. Nathan was no specialist in geology, but he could tell there was nothing of value here. Just an abandoned mine.

Disappointed, he traced his way back until he reached the place where the tunnel split. Well, if he was already here, why not search the other side? This one was larger, although there was nothing notable on the walls.

He didn't know how it happened. One step was on solid ground, the next went through the floor and he was falling into a shaft. When he reached the bottom, he took note of his surroundings. The mine shaft was not deep and he had not broken his legs, but it was smooth and he couldn't climb up.

He took out his knife. He always carried a knife with him, since his younger days in Santa Fe, New Mexico. It had served him well in countless situations. Of course, he could not carve the hard stone, but maybe he could create spaces to grab or to step on and make his way up.

A loud hissing sound at his feet caught his attention. With lighting fast instincts, honed by long years facing the enemy and unexpected dangers, he turned the light to the floor and in the same instant struck the snake at his feet.

Like in battle, he had no time think, only act. And just like then, looking at the dead snake, he felt his knees tremble like jello.

He cursed himself for venturing into this

abandoned mine alone. He knew his friends would come for him, but it was scary. He admitted it.

He pointed his flashlight up again to see if there was any rock that he could use to vault himself up. There was none. But what he saw made him blink. There was a solid vein of glittering mineral all around him. Copper was his guess, rich, almost pure.

Using his knife, he carved a piece out of the wall and placed it carefully in his pocket.

Just then, he heard a voice calling his name above.

"I'm here," he cried relieved.

From the bottom of the shaft, the sound was insulated and his voice barely made it to the surface. The person calling him went away, probably in the other tunnel. He could have cried in frustration.

"I'm here," he shouted at the top of his lungs.

Footsteps came closer. "Hold on Gunnery Sergeant, I'm throwing you a rope. I'm tying it to a post, but I'm not sure it will hold. The post is old and rotten."

Nathan knotted the rope at his waist, and taking

hold of it, he pulled himself up. When he was closer to the top, Dane grabbed his hand and pulled him all the way out of the shaft.

"Thank you," he told Dane after breathing deeply.

"We're not out of here yet."

At the entrance of the abandoned mine, they called for Connor. Another rope was dangling in the air. First Dane, then Nathan, were pulled up slowly, inch by torturous inch, out of the canyon.

Up on the rim, they just lied on the ground looking at the blue sky. Connor was patting his horse on the back for a job well done.

"Have you two had enough of exploring the unknown? Because I don't know about you, but I'm hungry."

"Yeah, let's go home," Nathan finally said, dusting his clothes.

"Did you find anything after all this trouble," Connor asked.

"Yeah, an old abandoned mine from one hundred years ago. I'm fairly sure this is what Coyote is looking for," Nathan answered him. "What I don't understand is how was he planning to remove the mineral. It's not his property."

"Did you find gold?" Connor joked in disbelief.

"No, no gold. I'm no expert, but there is a good vein of copper."

"Copper? Hmm. I think Coyote believes the property belongs to Richardson. He thinks he chased them away and plans to pay a measly sum for the property, if he finds the gold he believes is there," Dane said.

"Bingo! We found the answer." Nathan mounted his horse, happy to be alive and to breathe fresh air. "The rest is up to your father. I'll come next week at night to catch Coyote and his men in the act. Coyote is wanted for arson. Last month, he tried to burn Richardson's house. I think he only intended to scare them away. But arson is arson and Richardson has seen him and is witness."

CHAPTER 20

It was Saturday, early in the morning, and Nathan was having breakfast with his father and TJ Lomax on the small deck off the kitchen. Usually, all three of them woke up at the crack of dawn. It was perfect weather for the drive to Cheyenne that Nathan had planned for the day.

A whirlwind came through the gap in the fence. Joey was jumping up and down and couldn't contain his excitement. "We're going now, right. I want to see the gunfights and the rodeo." He climbed into Nathan's lap.

"Gunfights and rodeo, hmm? I wonder if your Mama will be as happy," TJ commented.

"She promised," Joey said, taken aback.

"It should be fun. I haven't seen a rodeo competition since I was very young, since my teenage days in Oklahoma," Nathan's father said, sipping his coffee.

"You could come with us, grandpa," little Joey suggested.

Nathan's coffee went down the wrong way and he had to cough. "Grandpa?" he croaked.

His father waved his hand dismissively. "All old men are called grandpa, don't you know?"

"He can come with us, can't he?" Joey persisted, one track-minded like all kids when they want to get their way.

How could Nathan object? "I guess so," he said with a marked lack of enthusiasm, but not because he objected to his father's presence. He'd hoped for a fun weekend with Laura and Joey, so they could bond as a family.

"Too bad dear Lydia can't come. She had knee replacement surgery in spring and is not entirely recovered."

Dear Lydia? Ah, right, Mrs. Taylor. Between Joey and his father, his family Saturday outing would change into a field trip for the whole neighborhood. In fact, his father turned to TJ.

"Not me." TJ forestalled him. "I have plans for this weekend. And I've seen the Frontier Days countless times. Don't forget to see the parade first."

Nathan was taking his wallet and keys from the dresser in his room and was ready to go, when his father came in.

"I'm ready," he said. "But I wanted to give you this." He placed on the dresser a single large sheet of paper unframed. "I made it yesterday."

It was a charcoal drawing, a portrait of Laura. It was a magnificent drawing that not only captured Laura's beauty, but also revealed her dreamy look from under long eyelashes, her sweetness, shyness mixed with fortitude, and the essence of her personality. His father had caught all this with just a few lines of charcoal, not an elaborate painting after long hours of sittings.

"You don't like it?" his father asked somewhat anxious.

"It's brilliant. I love it. I'll frame it next week." Nathan looked again in wonder at the portrait. "Tell me, if you can create such wonderful art, how could you waste your talent – pardon me for saying this – on those hideous paintings that you made for years?"

Instead of being upset, his father laughed. "At the time, I expressed my emotions on canvas. That's how I felt then. They reflected my talent in a different way. Now, I feel differently."

"What changed you?"

"Age. Understanding that every day is precious and should be enjoyed to the fullest. A serenity and acceptance of life the way it is."

The drive from Laramie to Cheyenne was not long, less than an hour. After leaving the truck in a crowded parking lot, they stopped under a large tree to watch the parade. Floats, marching bands, wagons with people in period costumes, riders.

Joey's eyes were wide in wonder absorbing everything that was going on around them. From time to time, Nathan lifted him up to see better. Street vendors were supplying the visitors with pancakes and hotdogs.

After an hour, they went to the Indian Village. There were booths with vendors of food and arts and crafts. Also free entertainment provided by a dance group from a reservation in central Wyoming. Joey was looking in awe at the colorful costumes and lively dancers. Nathan could barely take him away.

They ate fried bread and Nathan bought Laura a pair of delicate silver earrings from a local craftswoman. After he paid and was ready to go, the vendor stopped Nathan.

"Where are you from, boy?"

Surprised, Nathan almost dropped his purchase. "I was born in Oklahoma."

"Ah, Cherokee. You were lost for a long time, but you're returning home now. Good." She gave him a bracelet made of silver and turquoise beads. "For your woman. It matches her eyes and it's magical."

Laura was waiting for him outside. Joey was impatient to see the gun fighting and went ahead with Nathan's father.

Nathan handed her the earrings and the bracelet. She blushed with pleasure.

"Oh, you shouldn't have." She placed the earrings

in her ears immediately and looked at the bracelet. "It's so nice and beautiful. It's perfect for me."

"The vendor said it's magical."

"I hope it is. I need some magic in my life."

They found Joey and Nathan's father on a bench watching the gunfight re-enactments. Both the old man and the boy needed a break to rest their feet. He left Laura with them, and went to the nearby store selling western garb, and bought a large Stetson for his father and a smaller one for Joey. Then he returned to the re-enactment show. The hats were received with thanks and gladly tried on immediately. It was summer and quite warm, and the sun was shining brightly. His father had an old fashioned hat with narrow brim and Joey had lost the cap his mother had given him when they'd left home. Joey was especially proud of his new cowboy hat, turning his head this way and that, to be admired.

Nathan took a seat near them to watch the show. And he almost dropped the last piece of fry bread that he'd planned to savor. The sheriff in the re-enactment shouted at the villain and pulled his gun out very quickly.

Nathan's first thought was 'Wow! He is fast and good with guns.' The second was 'The sheriff looks like Lockhart. I'll be darned, it is Lockhart.'

Deputy Sheriff Brett Lockhart was playing the sheriff in the show, with such authenticity, making the drama so much more credible and real, that people applauded loudly and cheered for the hero.

What would it be like to be so sure of what you wanted to do in life, Nathan asked himself. Lockhart believed strongly in his mission on earth to be sheriff and chase the villains.

In the afternoon, the last stop of the day was the rodeo competition. Nathan worried that perhaps both Joey and his father were tired. He shouldn't have. Joey's eyes were sparkling with excitement and his father didn't look peaked at all. Very well, let's sit down and watch the competition, he thought.

First, there was calf roping and steer wrestling. Joey watched everything with interest and waved his new hat as he saw other people in the audience doing. Then the bronc riding started. Some of the competitors were

locals from the ranches around Cheyenne and Laramie.
And some were familiar figures.

"From Circle M ranch, Lucky Storm," the
announcer's voice boomed over the loud cheering of the
crowd.

"That is Raul Maitland's foreman," Nathan told
Laura.

"I met Raul and his wife Faith last Christmas,"
she answered.

Lucky was good, but unfortunately, the horse
he'd drawn was very wild, supplied by a local ranch
north of Cheyenne. He was bucked off before the eight
seconds were over. He dusted himself off and opened his
arms saying, "I did my best." Loud grumbles could be
heard from one side of the arena were the Maitland men
were sitting together.

"And now, please welcome Cory Malone, from
Diamond G ranch."

Cory was a youngster with some experience in
the rodeo circuit. A freak accident and the resulting
injury had tempered his desire to compete at the highest

level. He was Tom Gorman's man. He had a good horse, bucking enough to get a good score, but not a killer to get his rider injured. Cory lasted the entire eight second and received the second highest score.

"Good for him," Joey shouted above the loud cheering from the audience. A few other riders followed, some more lucky than others, but the first three highest scores held.

The noise was so loud that Nathan almost missed the announcer's words for the next to last rider. "From Bar M ranch, welcome Connor Monroe."

He couldn't be so crazy to compete with the younger cowboys, Nathan thought. But there was Connor, who was a rancher, not a rodeo rider, competing with the professionals. Nathan shook his head and prayed Connor would be safe.

Sensing his unease, Laura leaned toward him and squeezed his hand. "Do you know him?"

"Yeah, I do." What could he say? That Connor had just saved his life the day before? He watched tense Connor's descent into the chute on the horse's back and the attendant opening the gate. The horse exploded into the arena with Connor hanging on. He was a bad draw for Connor. Leaning back at the horse's every bucking, his left hand in the air, the right one gripping the bridle, Connor continued to hold on in the saddle.

Eight long seconds seemed endless. When the bell sounded, Connor vaulted down and the crowd burst into loud applauses and cheers.

Against all odds, Connor Monroe had won the bronc riding competition, defeating riders more experienced than him.

CHAPTER 21

Nathan had a plan and he went to talk to the sheriff about it.

"Jack, I want to go tonight to catch Coyote and his gang. They didn't do anything illegal, except for trespassing and digging in the canyon. But it's been an unusually dry summer and the ranchers are getting antsy with all the fires lit at night. A spark in the dried grass and we could have wildfire engulfing this whole area. Not to mention that cowboys are superstitious and they don't like the unholy fires popping up at night."

Jack leaned back in his chair. "Coyote is wanted for arson and don't forget that he or one of his men attacked Iris' grandfather in his house. Yes, they have to be stopped. Did you find out what they want?"

"I think so. There is an entrance into an abandoned mine in the wall of the canyon. There is a good copper vein there. Of course, the copper belongs to Monroe. It's on his land. Even if they find it, there is no way they could mine the copper. So, I'm not sure what they intend to do."

"Hmm." Jack sipped from his ever present coffee mug. "It is possible they think the land still belongs to Richardson. They chased the old man away. Maybe they want to be sure there is copper – or perhaps they think there is gold – and then make him a low offer for the property."

"Yeah, maybe so. I'm going tonight with Dane to catch them."

"You said that there were tire tracks. The only way out by car from what is now the Monroe side of the canyon is by crossing the old bridge."

"What bridge?"

"Farther away, the canyon is not so deep, and there is an old bridge that practically no one uses now. That is the only road and it leads to Richardson's house. It is possible they are holed up there because the house is vacant."

Nathan shook his head. "If so, then why don't they search the canyon from that side?"

"The tall boulders behind Richardson's house

make access to the canyon almost impossible. I'll drive tonight with Cole on the road that leads to Richardson's house. It's a gamble. But if I'm right, then we can cut off their only way to retreat. Be careful."

Nathan went to talk to Deputy Lockhart. He'd made a promise and a Marine never goes back on his word.

"We're going tonight?" Lockhart's eyes sparkled with glee. "Ah, we'll catch them, we'll smash them, we'll…"

"Remember, no gun shots to scare them away," Nathan cautioned him.

"No, of course not. We'll be as quiet as church mice."

They met a little after ten at night at Monroe's ranch house. Nathan introduced Lockhart to Dane and Connor.

"McRavy? Are you related to our sheriff?" Lockhart asked.

"I'm his brother."

Lockhart looked him up and down appraisingly. "Another hero soldier?"

Dane stiffened. "I'm not a soldier. Technically, I'm a sailor, because I'm a Navy SEAL. I'm retired now."

"Do you plan to hire as a Deputy too?"

"No, not me. I plan to raise horses."

Lockhart cheered up. "Good, good. Not everybody can be a good sheriff. Do you know how to shoot?"

Dane looked at him amused. "Yeah, you could say that. I am a SEAL. I had sniper training."

"Good. What about you?" Lockhart turned to Connor Monroe.

"I'm a rancher. I can shoot a mountain lion at two hundred feet with my rifle." Connor answered patting his rifle that was already in a scabbard on his saddle.

But Lockhart was not paying attention to him anymore. He was looking mesmerized at a young woman crying on the porch.

"Who is that?" Nathan asked.

"That is Rachel. Dad decided his first grandson can't live in poverty, so he brought them both here. You were right. The boy is mine. I'll raise him. Rachel… is another story. I'm not going to marry her."

Meanwhile, Lockhart had approached her and was patting her awkwardly on the shoulder.

Rachel raised her teary eyes to him and laid a hand on his chest. "You are so brave and you are such a comfort to me."

Connor rolled his eyes in disgust. "Do you think he'll fall for her antics?"

"Hook, line, and sinker," Dane answered dryly.

The ride to the canyon took about half an hour. They thought they'd be early, but the fire could be seen from far away.

"They are bent on starting a wildfire," Connor grumbled.

They stopped at a distance where Nathan hoped they wouldn't be seen.

"I'll try to get closer and see what they are doing," Nathan told the others.

"I'm with you," Dane said, strapping his shotgun to his back, with an easiness that showed a lot of practice.

In the end, they left the horses with Connor's man and the four of them made their way slowly and silently. It was full moon and there was plenty of light.

Dane pointed out to Nathan that one of Coyote's men was lowered over the rim into the canyon on a thick rope.

"I'll try to get closer to the man with a paper in his hand. I think that's Coyote. If I catch him, then the others will surrender without a fight."

He didn't have a chance to do it. Lockhart had been unusually quiet until then, but emboldened by having been admired by a pretty woman, he rose from behind the rocks where they were hiding.

"This is the sheriff. You are surrounded. Come out with your hands up." And then he fired above their heads.

The result was not what he had expected. The outlaws dropped everything, including the man who had been lowered into the canyon, and ran away in the opposite direction. Coyote fired a gun toward them, but without much precision.

Lockhart fired after them and a cry of pain confirmed he'd hit one of them. That didn't stop them. There were four of them. They reached a truck that was parked farther away.

As Jack had said earlier, they made an abrupt left turn to cross the canyon on the old bridge.

"Let's go back to take the horses," Nathan said. "And we have to put out the fires before they spread. It will slow us down, but Jack is cutting off their retreat so they have nowhere to run."

By the time they finished with the fires, a cursing man vaulted himself above the rim of the canyon. "Darn them to leave me dangling above the abyss and to run away without me."

"You are under arrest," Lockhart proclaimed, pulling out the handcuffs from his belt.

"Wait, Lockhart," Nathan said. "Let him tell us about Coyote's plans."

The man was genuinely peeved to have been left behind. "He promised us equal parts of the treasure, but I doubt he was going to keep his word. He wanted to trick us all to do the hard work digging at the bottom of the canyon. He'd have left us high and dry."

"What treasure? Do you mean you thought there was gold in the old mine?" Connor asked.

The man looked back at him dumbfounded. "I don't know of any mine. Coyote has a map with the location of the Lamont treasure."

"The Lamont treasure? And you people believed him? That is a kid's game. A treasure hunt. All boys love to search for it."

"Coyote had an old map."

"Pshaw!" Connor scoffed. "There are treasure maps everywhere, even at the county fair. Any crook can sell to you a fake map."

"I haven't seen it. Coyote didn't show it to us. But he said he had it authenticated by an expert in old documents from Denver. He said the treasure is here in this place in the canyon. It's true that all the digging was for nothing. We haven't found it yet."

"Why the fires?"

"Coyote is superstitious. It's a ritual. Like a guiding light or something. I didn't mind the hot coffee though, after a night of digging in the hard rock."

"It figures. Fire ritual. The man is an arsonist," Nathan concluded.

"He sure is," Dane agreed. "Look, he lit a fire on the other side of the canyon." He pointed in that direction. From behind the tall boulders, a wavy trail of smoke rose on the canopy of the dark night sky.

"That's right in Richardson's back yard," Nathan said. The smoke trail thickened, and he looked at Dane horrified. "You don't think Coyote set fire to the house?" There was no time to waste. "Lockhart, you and Connor's man take this man to the ranch house and then take him to jail in the cruiser. We'll ride over the bridge to see what's burning."

Nathan didn't wait to see if Lockhart protested

his order.

He mounted his horse, and went to cross the old bridge, together with Connor and Dane.

When they reached Richardson's house on the other side of the canyon, they found a scene right out of 'The Inferno'. The house was burning and there was no one else there. Nathan dismounted and took his frightened horse to the barn, which was the only structure untouched by the fire. He knew Richardson had a well, so that he could water his wife's vegetable garden in the short growing season. He uncoiled the hose and prayed that it would work. It did.

The water from the hose was no match to the roaring fire, but people fought fire with whatever they had at hand, including buckets.

Nathan hoped that Jack had caught Coyote and his gang. He looked with regret at the old house. This had been a hundred year old homestead, added on with every generation. It's true that it was empty now. Richardson had removed his furniture and all his personal items when he had moved to town. He intended to sell the house. But perhaps another family would have enjoyed it for years to come, and built a life and memories here.

Now there were only ashes left.

CHAPTER 22

Nathan had no idea how much time had passed. Mindlessly, he pumped water with the hose into the burning house.

"The firefighters are here. Jack called them," Dane informed him.

"Did he catch Coyote?" Nathan wanted to know.

"Yeah. He got them all and took them to jail." Dane's eye patch was askew and he was dirty with soot. He had found another outdoor faucet and some flower pots. He and Connor had used those. They had not been very effective, but the firefighters praised them for stopping the fire from spreading to the dry grass.

"This was a good house," Nathan said looking with regret at the blackened skeleton of the house, nestled at the base of the boulders bordering the canyon. "It's such a pity." He stepped inside to look at what remained of the house. Not much. Some posts and beams, half charred. The rest was almost all gone, except for the massive stone fireplace. That was still there, covered in soot, but erect like a monument in the middle of a ruin.

"You and I have seen destruction that was a lot worse than this. You'd think we would be used to such images. But it still breaks my heart to see such senseless loss," Dane said, wandering around the ruined structure with his flashlight. "It can be rebuilt. It was a solid construction. Look at this fireplace. It still looks intact."

"It's covered in soot," Nathan observed.

"A little water and soap can restore it to its former glory," Dane said, rubbing his hand over the stones above the blackened mantel.

"I doubt Richardson will ever rebuild, even if he is insured," Nathan said tired and ready to go home to wash and sleep.

"Hmm, what a pity. This is a grand fireplace."

"Who cares? I don't think Richardson will succeed to find a buyer crazy enough to live here so far from town, and without land to make a good ranch. But if he does, the new owner might demolish everything and build a new contemporary house with an electric fireplace with plaster all around."

"That would be a pity," Dane said looking at the stone fireplace. "It has so much character."

"You could buy it," Nathan suggested and stepped back.

"Watch out," Dane shouted and pulled him to the side. A beam that had supported the roof, fell and hit Nathan in the back, disintegrating in several smoldering pieces. "Are you okay?"

"I think so. It's the second time you saved my life. If you had not pulled me aside, it would have hit my head. But instead, it only grazed my back and singed my shirt."

One of the firefighters came in to tell them they were leaving. "Hey men, it's not safe to stay here. The fire is extinguished, but it's still dangerous." He looked at Nathan. "What happened to you? You have some scrapes and minor burns. We'll take you to the hospital."

So, instead of going home, Nathan landed in the hospital, where an army of nurses and doctors took care of him. They undressed him, cleaned his wounds, took his blood pressure, and checked his eyes, his lungs, and heart.

In the beginning, he was embarrassed about them seeing his scared abdomen, but he was given a hospital gown tied in the back over his pants. His shirt was worse than a rag and smelled of smoke.

Dane had promised to come in an hour to drive him home.

A very pretty nurse was taking his blood pressure, again. Had it changed from ten minutes ago?

The door opened and a frazzled-looking Laura entered the room. "I'll take care of him," she told the other one tersely.

"But you are from pediatrics," the other nurse objected.

"He's my fiancé. Go," Laura ordered her.

The other nurse narrowed her eyes, "I'll report…"

"You do that," Laura closed the door behind her. Then came back to Nathan and looked at him. "When I heard you were hurt, I thought I'd go crazy. I was told your wounds are not life-threatening. Where are you hurt?"

"On my back. A burning beam fell, but Dane pulled me to safety."

She checked his back slowly, professionally. Then she sat down near him. Her eyes filled with tears. When life was rough, his sweet Laura showed weakness and tears, but also professional competence and strength to do what needed to be done. And he loved her just the way she was, a delicate flower you thought would be destroyed by the first storm, only to surprise you by surviving and blooming even more profusely.

"Do you know what scared me the most?" she asked between sobs. "That I allowed my unreasonable fear to dominate my life and I didn't have the courage to tell you the truth. I love you Nathan and I can't imagine life without you. It was like someone told me, 'What are you waiting for, girl? Life will pass you by and Nathan will leave you.'"

"No, never. I'll never leave you, Laura. You are

everything that is good, sweet, and beautiful in my life. I've seen so much ugliness and violence. I need you."

She looked at him shyly from under her lashes. "Does this mean you'll marry me?"

"Oh, yes. I'm yours forever."

Nathan bent to kiss her, when the door opened and a man in a white coat came in. He looked like he was about to explode. "What is going on here?"

Nathan sighed. How imposing could he appear, undressed and clutching to his chest a hospital gown with tiny pink flowers on it? "I was hurt while on duty and my fiancée came in to check on me." He read the name embroidered on the front of the white coat, Dr. David Jones. Ah, so this was the infamous Dr. Jones.

"Not in the hospital. It is not allowed for personnel to consort with patients." The next words got stuck in the doctor's throat.

Nathan had risen from the chair, trying to even the confrontation. The gown slipped from his hands and the doctor saw his abdominal scars. Dr. Jones was a surgeon, and he had a very good idea of how badly

Nathan must have been injured to require so much surgery.

"Are you a soldier?"

"I'm a Marine. I was discharged. Now I work as Deputy Sheriff here in town."

They could read nothing on the doctor's face. He nodded. "Take care," he said and left without another word.

In the evening, Dane McRavy came to see Nathan at home. "I have news," he announced.

They went out on the deck where TJ and Nathan's father were playing cribbage. Joey was chasing after his dog in the yard.

"Let's sit here. I have news too." Nathan poured them iced tea. It was a balmy evening, not too hot under the trees that shaded the deck. "This is a life of leisure. Peaceful."

"Tell me your news first," Dane demanded sipping the iced-tea and thinking a cold beer would make life perfect indeed.

"I got engaged to Laura."

"Buddy, the whole town already knows this news."

"Well, that was… never mind. What's your news? I hope Coyote didn't escape again."

"No, he didn't. He's still enjoying the hospitality of our county jail. My news is also personal."

"You're getting married too?" Nathan asked joking.

"No, of course not. I'm a confirmed bachelor. Besides, who would want me? I look rather scary, or so I've been told." Dane pulled his chair closer to Nathan's and refilled his glass from the pitcher on the table. "I went to see Richardson today."

"Poor man. How did he take the news that his old family home burned down completely?"

"Not too bad. He'd already moved out with all his belongings, and he has insurance." Dane looked at the darkening sky. "I bought the place from him, as you advised me to do."

"You did what? I was… I don't know what I was

thinking. The house is destroyed." Nathan was worried that his new friend had made a mistake. He had been joking when he'd told him to buy the property.

"I can rebuild the house the way I want and I have the fireplace as a starting point. Richardson asked a fair price for the land only. He will get the insurance money for the house. We both win. I told him about the copper vein and the abandoned mine on the land sold to Monroe. I had to tell him that the canyon is basically a rupture in the earth from geological times. It is probable that his side of the canyon, where the old house was, has an equally rich vein of mineral that has not yet been discovered."

"Monroe doesn't want to mine it. He wants to preserve the land the way it is for ranching. At least for now. What did Richardson say?"

"Pretty much the same. He's not interested in selling it to a mining company for more money. He is happy that his place will remain in the family."

"What family?"

"Me. I'm part of his family now. Jack is married

to his granddaughter, and I'm Jack's brother."

Nathan raised his finger. "True. These pills are making me slow-minded. I'm glad you decided to stay in the area. However, the place is out of the way."

Dane shrugged. "It suits me. It's not far from town, only about thirty minutes. I like that it is isolated. I'm excited about starting work on my house. I can already picture it in my mind. The exterior will be like the old house, with the same character and charm. Richardson gave me some pictures. Inside, it will be larger, with an open-floor plan. The barn is in good shape and quite spacious. In time, I'll have to build a second outbuilding for a workshop, for my restoration business."

It was good to see the somber Navy SEAL so animated, Nathan thought. Both of them were caught up in their civilian lives, planning for the future. Both of them were healing, not only their bodies, but also their wounded souls.

CHAPTER 23

The doorbell rang just when Nathan was ready to go to work in the afternoon. He was on duty until midnight.

He opened the door. "Yes," he answered tersely.

On the front porch, there was a middle aged gentleman, dressed in a suit, albeit rumpled, with a red bow tie at his neck. He looked out of place in this town, where everyone preferred jeans and plaid shirts. He was like a fish out of water.

"Is this Simon Young's house?" he asked in an officious and haughty manner.

"No, it's not. But he sleeps here on the couch in the living room."

"Can I speak with him?"

"Not now. He is in the park with Joey and the dog. He should be back soon." What lunatic had his father brought here? And for what purpose? – Nathan wondered.

"Could I wait for him here? I need to sit down.

The commuter flight from Denver to Laramie was horrendous. It made me queasy."

"Of course. Could you please tell me who are you?" Nathan asked guiding the man to the outdoor deck. He figured that a queasy man should be closer to nature, just in case.

"I'm his investment banker," the man said absently, setting his briefcase carefully on the deck, and wiping the iron wrought chair with a pristine white handkerchief.

Do handkerchiefs still exist? And who buys them, when a tissue box is more practical? Then the man's words resonated in his mind. "You said investment banker?"

He knew it. He just knew it. His father was embroiled in a crooked financial scheme and had to go into hiding. Where better, if not here, making him Nathan's responsibility. And now, the investment people had caught up with him.

The doorbell rang again. He went to answer. At front of the door, with his finger poised to ring again, there was a younger version of the banker. The same pin striped suit, white shirt, assorted with a blue tie. He carried an expensive leather briefcase in his hand.

"Is Simon Young available?"

"No. He's in the park with Joey and the dog. You just missed him. He had to come back to take the bag for the dog."

"The bag for the dog?" the other man repeated dumbfounded.

"For the dog's business. We are a civilized town here." Jeez, these people didn't have dogs? Nathan was losing his patience.

"Is he going to be late with this dog business?"

"No, he'll be back soon."

"May I wait for him inside, please?"

Nathan sighed. "Sure. Go on the deck and sit with the other one," he said pointing to the open door to the deck. "And by the way, who are you?"

"I'm Mr. Young's lawyer."

It figures, after the whole investment disaster, his dear Dad needed a lawyer to save him from trouble.

Nathan was ruminating this new complication in his life, when the doorbell rang again. Sure enough, another suit at the door; this one older.

"Simon Young?"

"He's not here now, but you can wait on the deck with the others."

The man entered mindful of his briefcase, like he carried the code to a secret weapon.

"And who are you?" Nathan asked after him.

"I'm his financial advisor."

"Very funny. To advise him of what? How to clip coupons for the grocery store?"

"Ha-ha. Very funny indeed," the man answered dryly before stepping out on the deck. It seemed sense of humor was not a requirement in order to be a financial advisor.

There was no way Nathan could go to work until midnight without knowing what was going on. He walked out on the deck. The three men were sitting with their suitcases at their feet one near the other.

"Look, I'm a Deputy Sheriff and I'm his son. If

dear Dad is in trouble, then I'd like to know now. I have a right to know because he came to me."

The three suits looked at each other, then at him. The lawyer said, "Why should he be in trouble? As far as I know, he's not in any legal trouble."

"His investments are in perfect order," the banker added.

"His finances couldn't be any better," the advisor of some sort nodded with utmost gravity.

All right. Nathan could breathe more easily. However, this didn't explain their presence here. "I'm glad, extremely glad, to hear there is no trouble. So why are you here?"

They looked at him like he was slow minded. "To give him his monthly report, of course," the lawyer answered.

"He was supposed to meet us in New York as usual, but he announced at the last minute that he couldn't make it. We had to fly all the way here instead," the banker said peeved. It looked like he was over his queasiness.

Nathan looked at his watch. It was late, very late. "I have to go. I'm on duty till midnight tonight. But when I come back, I'll get to the bottom of this."

They looked at him warily as he strapped his gunbelt to his middle. "You sit there until he comes back, you hear?" Nathan looked at them and the three of them nodded in unison.

Nathan could hardly wait to finish his work and go home. A deposition in Judge Fontayne's Court in the afternoon didn't improve his mood.

"What's wrong with you?" Deputy Lockhart asked him. "We caught the bad guys with arson. The ranchers are happy and praise us. Why are you moody? The beautiful Laura doesn't want you anymore?"

"Don't hold your breath. I got news for you. The beautiful Laura agreed to marry me," Nathan barked at him annoyed.

"The whole town already knows this news. Then what? Are you afraid I'll beat you in the shooting competition? By the way, I invited the Navy SEAL to take part too. The winner will be proclaimed the best shooter in the county."

"Lockhart, this is a bad idea for you. Dane had sniper training. He is likely to hit the target one hundred per cent of the time."

"We'll see," Lockhart smiled with superiority.

Because he couldn't stand the suspense of what was going on at home, Nathan change his last six hours with Cole who was supposed to come at midnight.

When he arrived home, Nathan discovered that the three men had left. His father was on the deck, telling Joey a story about a boy and his dog in Alaska. TJ was frowning at some papers he was perusing. It was another peaceful summer evening. He needed a larger house for his family, Nathan thought. But first, he had to tackle whatever trouble his father had.

"Dad, we need to talk," he said as he took a seat in one of the chairs.

His father patted Joey on the back. "We'll continue this story tomorrow."

Joey sighed. "Is this one of the grown-up talks where I have to go brush my teeth so as not to hear?"

Nathan laughed. The boy was witty and quick. He loved him. "No, Joey. In our house, children are included in the talk. Now, Dad, this morning three men in suits came here looking for you. They swore that you are not in any trouble. But I'd like you to tell me honestly what is going on."

It was the first time since his father had come knocking on his door that Nathan looked at him carefully. His father appeared old and thin. Maybe they should postpone this talk…

His father started talking. "My luck changed eleven years ago. One of the art dealers in New York City - one of many to whom I used to send my paintings - was ready to return the package to me unopened, as all of them usually did. However, that day he had to go to one of his wealthy art collectors with three paintings from famous artists. It was supposed to be one of those transactions where a lot of value and money changed hands."

"And what did he do?" Joey asked, his eyes wide with interest.

"He took the three paintings. In his haste, he also grabbed by mistake the box with my painting, which was under the other three, waiting to be taken to the post office. His client was not in a good mood that day and the dealer knew the sale would be difficult. He smiled and presented his three paintings, hoping the client would buy at least one. No such luck. The collector mumbled and grumbled and didn't like any of them, telling the dealer that he'd wasted his time."

"But then he saw yours…" Joey anticipated.

"Yes. He pointed to the unopened box and asked what was in it. The dealer was in a dilemma. If he presented a low quality painting, then his reputation would be doomed. But not selling anything would be worse. The collector might go to another dealer. He was shrewd and said that it was a painting by a relatively unknown genius, requested by another collector. The client demanded to see it."

"And he loved it." Joey anticipated, jumping with

glee.

Nathan was afraid to ask, "Was it one of the many angry ladies you painted?"

"Yeah. Something similar. More abstract and more bold. Striking in black and red. Anyhow, he was impressed. And here comes the funny part. Thinking this was New York City and I had to be taken seriously, I attached to it a tag with a price of three thousand."

"Good Lord, Dad. You've never even sold a painting for three... hundred dollars. We lived from paintings with flowers and adobe houses you sold to tourists for fifty dollars."

His father smiled. "Yes. The art collector looked at it and said, 'Pricey, but well worth the money.' And he wrote a check for three million dollars."

"Whaat?" Nathan stared at his father open-mouthed.

His father nodded. "Yes. These are the prices serious dealers ask in New York City. The rest is history – as they say. My paintings started selling, fetching high prices. My name became famous in the art world. I bought a loft in New York City for convenience. But I invested most of my money and made quite a fortune. In other words, I'm rich."

"What does it mean?" Joey asked. "Does it mean we can buy fancy dog food for Robbie? Mama said our dog has such fancy taste and eats so much, that we'll be poor."

Nathan was stunned. He'd never expected this. Not in his wildest dreams. His father, the bohemian artist, was a millionaire. "But if you don't need my help, then why did you come to see me?"

His father looked at him sadly. "I guess I deserve this question. I want you to know that I worried about you every day after you went to war."

"But not enough to come see me when I was in the hospital and the doctors were not sure if I'd survive another day."

"I couldn't. You see, there is more to the story. Last year, I was diagnosed with lung cancer."

"How is this possible? You've never smoked."

"It happens. It was right before my surgery when

I heard about you being wounded. Then I needed radiation and chemotherapy. Bad timing. I'm sorry."

"What does this mean, grandpa?" Joey asked looking from one to the other without understanding.

"It means that I'm in remission now and I'm going to live longer. What do you say about that, young Joey?" he said tickling the boy and making him laugh.

"Great. I think that's great."

CHAPTER 24

Nathan was holding Laura in his arms, sitting on the bench under the old rose arbor in Mrs. Taylor's yard.

"Laura, we have to get married soon, or I'll go crazy from wanting you. I'm not a teenager to steal kisses from my girlfriend in the backyard, under the suspicious eyes of the parents," Nathan complained, his mouth trailing kisses on Laura's neck and making her shiver in a satisfactory way. He was still amazed that such a beautiful creature like Laura had agreed to marry him.

She giggled. "There is only one parent, your father, and he can't be called 'suspicious'. On the contrary, in case you haven't noticed, he's matchmaking."

"Is he? Well, at least, he's doing one thing right." Nathan was lost, inhaling Laura's sweet flowery fragrance that was uniquely hers. "Let's elope," he suggested, busy kissing the soft skin below her ear.

"No."

Her denial sobered him. "Did you change your mind?"

She cupped his cheek. "No, of course not. But I eloped once. It was a hasty decision and the whole marriage was a disaster. I want to do it right this time. Not in grand style with a lot of expense, although your father offered to pay an outrageous amount. You'll see I'm a thrifty girl. I want a nice, proper wedding in church, surrounded by all our friends. Not many guests. I'll invite my brother Joe from Colorado Springs and you can ask your relatives from Oklahoma."

"Then you'll have a lot of guests. On a whim, I wrote to my cousin Nelson in Oklahoma. He emailed me back immediately. Dad was right. The younger generation doesn't hold grudges like the old one. After grandpa died, the family tried to reach me, but I was in Afghanistan, and I never received their messages. Cousin Nelson eagerly agreed to come to my wedding and assured me that so will the rest of the family, all seventy-six of them."

"Seventy-six?"

"Yep. You see, your small wedding will spiral out of control as they usually do," Nathan observed, hoping that she'd see eloping in a better light.

"Well, okay then. I wanted to keep the expenses under control. In that case, I'll have to accept your father's offer to help."

"You're not serious. Do you want all of Oklahoma to invade us?"

She smiled at him. Her blue eyes were bright sapphires in the dim light of the yard. "They are your family, Nathan. It will be a splendid wedding. The entire county will talk about it."

"That is what I'm afraid of."

"I want Joey to be included in the ceremony and my friend from work, Emmy, to be my maid of honor. I assume you want Jack as your best man...."

"Jack is a wonderful man and a good friend. I'll always owe him for making me stop in this town and take the deputy job. But his brother Dane is a military man like me and I feel a kinship with him. We understand each other. Dane will be my best man."

"All right." Laura's laughter sounded like a tinkling bell and they continued making plans for their future together long into the night.

The upstairs window closed quietly. The old man turned to his friend smiling. "I'll be forever grateful that you called me to come here, TJ. Thank you, my friend."

* * *

Keep reading for an excerpt from *Misty Meadow At Dawn*, Book 3 of the Summer Days In Wyoming series, Dane's story.

Misty Meadows

At Dawn

VIVIAN SINCLAIR

CHAPTER 1

Dane McRavy came home late in the evening. It had been a hot summer day and he was dusty, although happy that the work at his new house was progressing nicely. Once inside, he saw his landlord Good Old Bill Sanders snoring softly on the couch in the living room, while his favorite show about aliens was on TV with the volume at maximum. Good Old Bill couldn't hear as well as in his youth, but he was too proud to have himself fitted with a hearing aid.

Smiling, Dane pulled off his eyepatch, which had chafed his skin all day. He needed a shower and food. Surprisingly, Good Old Bill had mastered cooking some dishes. Because Good Old Bill didn't want to accept rent money from him, Dane gave him a generous allowance for food and utilities. The arrangement worked well for both of them until Dane's house would be ready, before the first snowfall, he hoped.

He opened the door to his room, when he saw that the bathroom door was cracked open and a sliver of light came through. Who could be in the bathroom? This neighborhood of smaller, less expensive houses had become quite run down in recent years due to some unsavory characters who were involved in crime.

His instincts honed in the twenty years he'd spent as a Navy SEAL, Dane pushed the door open slowly, quietly. Then he froze in the doorway.

A mermaid rose from the antique claw-footed tub, like Venus from the sea, water sluicing down her beautiful body. Gracefully, she caught an errant curl and arranged it back into her loose topknot. Then she grabbed the towel from the rack and wiped her face. She blinked and seeing Dane, she shrieked like a banshee.

"Help, Daddy! Call the police…" She covered herself with the towel continuing in the same shrill voice, "No, don't come any closer. I'm armed. I'll shoot you."

Somehow, this struck Dane as funny. "Will you?" Then he realized that his eyepatch was missing and she was looking with horror at his damaged face. He sobered. "Sorry for intruding. The door was open." He left closing the door carefully behind him.

He was searching for a new shirt in the drawer,

2

when Good Old Bill knocked on the door. "My daughter Emma came unexpectedly from Denver and she had no idea who you were. I'm sorry."

Dane forced himself to smile reassuringly. "I thought there was an intruder in the bathroom. No problem. I apologize. I'll look for a room at a motel."

"No, no. It's not necessary. There are three bedrooms and I explained to Emma that I feel safer with you here."

What could he say? He did not want to offend this generous old man who had welcomed him to live in his home rent-free. "All right. But I'll leave if your daughter is uncomfortable with my presence here."

In the end, he showered quickly and left father and daughter have dinner together while he went to Kate's diner. The truck stop out of town was unusually crowded that evening, but he found an empty booth in the back, near the kitchen.

Kate herself came out of the kitchen to greet him. "How are you, soldier? Or did you turn cowboy now?"

He smiled at the tall, middle-aged woman. "Not

yet, but I will."

"How is the Marine? He didn't come Thursdays for our meatloaf."

"Nathan is getting married."

"Ah, that explains it. What can I bring you?"

"Whatever is your Today Special, Kate. I'm not fussy."

She nodded and left him to his thoughts. He looked around. It was a rowdy place, but he was at ease here and loved Kate's food. The smell from the kitchen was appetizing, unlike the burned oil from some greasy spoons.

The kitchen door opened and the helper, Minnie, came out with a steaming large plate. She set it down in front of him. "It's stew. Today's Special. It's really good. I hope you like it." She smiled at him shyly.

"Thank you. Do you have to serve because Kate is short staffed?" He was uneasy about this slip of a girl serving the burly truckers from the other tables.

"No. Hannah is serving. I only brought you the food."

"Can you stay with me five minutes?" he asked between delicious bites of stew.

Minnie bit her lip, then nodded, and squeezed on the opposite bench. "But only five minutes. It's been busy and I have to wash the dishes."

Dane observed that her hands were chapped and red. She also had a bruise on her wrist. "Your hands are hurt because of washing dishes. Maybe I should tell Kate not to…."

"No, please don't tell her. She is good to me and I need the work. The redness is from doing laundry at home. Our washing machine is broken and I have to do it by hand."

Dane had never heard of anyone washing clothes by hand in this day and age. "Then it needs to be fixed."

"Dad is a bit short of money for the moment."

"Is it just you and your father?" Maybe the father was sick and she had to support them both. That might explain it.

"And my three brothers." She seemed embarrassed and changed the subject. "Do you still have the lucky penny I gave you?"

"Sure. Right here." He patted his shirt pocket. "Do you want it back?"

"No, no. You keep it and don't give it away. It will bring you luck. I have to go now." She rose and went back to the kitchen. She turned in the doorway to look at him again. "Come back, please. I'll miss you if you don't."

In the light above the door, he saw that she had lovely cornflower blue eyes with long dark eyelashes.

"I will," he promised. He looked after her as she disappeared in the kitchen. Something was wrong. She had a father and three brothers, but none of them were able to fix the washing machine or buy a new one.

He shook his head. It was not his business, but he couldn't stop thinking of the little sparrow of a girl and her plight in life.

He fingered the lucky penny and remembered his military career that had ended abruptly, and how it had all started.

MISTY MEADOWS AT DAWN

Twenty years ago, on a small ranch near Lampasas, Texas

"What do you mean, Lucy left? What did she say, Mom?" Seventeen year old Dane McRavy was pacing the kitchen in deep turmoil.

"She said she is not going to spend her life with a poor rancher like you." His mother kept stirring in the big pot on the stove. "Face it son, she left you high and dry. She said she's going to Dallas where she has relatives and she'll never return to this small town."

Dane stopped and faced his mother. "I don't understand. We had plans. I was accepted to college and I am going to get a degree in agricultural studies before coming back here to work the land. She agreed to marry me."

"You just finished high school, Dane. You're too young to talk of marriage. This is your proof. The flighty girl changed her mind after all. This should be a lesson to you."

"No, no. You must have misunderstood. Lucy

would never leave me." Agitated, Dane went out the door, climbed in his old truck, and drove to town, where his girlfriend Lucinda lived.

He left the truck in front of her house and knocked on the front door. Lucy's father answered.

"What do you want?" He was not very friendly, but Dane was too upset to care.

"I need to speak to Lucy. Please Mr. Gardner."

"Lucinda is going to Dallas to live with her aunt. She doesn't want to talk to you."

"No, she can't do that. We had plans. She agreed." Dane told him.

"If she did, then she changed her mind. She doesn't want to talk to you."

Dane shook his head vehemently. "She couldn't change her mind. I don't believe it."

"Believe it," Lucy's voice confirmed, from the top of the stairs.

Dane looked up at her. Her face was chalk-white and she was gripping the railing, but her voice was steady. "Lucy," he cried distraught. "What about our

8

plans?"

"Your mother explained to me what your family's expectations are."

"What about us?"

"There is no us, Dane. Go home and don't come back." She turned her back on him and entered her room closing her door.

"You heard her, boy. Go away now." Lucy's father pushed him and closed the door in his stunned face.

Dane raised his fist to knock again, only to realize it was pointless. Lucy had broken up with him and there was nothing he could do to change her mind. And with her, all his plans went down the drain.

He drove aimlessly through town. He couldn't return home. There was nothing for him there. No Lucy, no future. He had no idea what to do.

He stopped in the town square and parked his truck. A small diner cross the street attracted his attention. He was not hungry, although he hadn't eaten anything all day. But he was thirsty, very thirsty.

Distracted, he started to cross the road to go to the diner. A dark car drove around the corner at high speed and almost knocked him down. A strong arm pulled him back just in the nick of time.

"Well son, if you are so intent on killing yourself at least do it for a noble cause."

Dane looked at the tall man dressed in military uniform, who pointed to a small office, right near the florist. 'Navy Recruitment Center'.

Sometimes when you don't know what to do in life, providence shows you the way, Dane thought. "Yes, I'll do it," he said.

"Are you sure?" the military man asked him.

Dane was determined and he signed the enlistment papers. He returned home later that night, with the papers in his pocket. He packed a duffel bag and a few clean clothes. As an afterthought, he threw inside a tattered copy of his favorite book Gary Paulsen's "Hatchet", and a picture of him with his younger brother Jack, both of them grinning at their father who was taking the picture. That was it.

He wrote on a piece of paper - "I enlisted in the Navy. I'll keep you posted, Dane". Then he looked around the room where he'd grown up and he left the house without saying Good-bye. He left behind his childhood and all his naïve hopes and plans.

The Navy accepted him immediately and he was sent to training camp after his physical exam. Many other enlisted men had trouble and found the tests difficult, but Dane excelled. Not because he was in better shape or more ambitious, but because he didn't care or fear. He didn't have to push himself. He just did what he was ordered to do, without thinking of himself.

And so he was commended and promoted and became part of the elite corps that was the Navy SEALs. He was very good and efficient at what he did.

Did he ever regret his decision to enlist? No. This was his life and he had a lot of satisfaction for a job well done. He didn't regret it even when he received news from his parents that the ranch that was supposed to have been his inheritance, had been sold and his parents had moved to Austin.

He missed his brother, Jack. He heard that after seven years with Dallas Police Department, Jack quit abruptly leaving for parts unknown. Or so his mother told him. He was not sure how credible she was.

Lucy wrote to him several years later. Her letter came to him through his father, about six months after it was written. He read it with interest, but without any emotion. Lucy explained that his mother told her to go away because Dane was too young to know his own mind, that he had a ranch to take care of, and that he was not getting married. He suspected something like that had occurred, but now it was too late to turn back the clock. What was the point? Lucy was married and was expecting her second child. Life went on.

Dane had his busy exciting life and was happy to be a Navy SEAL. Despite his courage and being known as a risk-taker, he had never been severely wounded. He became a legendary hero among the SEALs.

Until one day, when a carefully planned mission went awry, and he was badly wounded. The SEALs carried him back to safety, and he was happy to be alive.

But he knew his life in dangerous combat zones was finished.

The army surgeons patched up his face the best they could, but were unable to save his left eye. He also had a titanium rod in his left leg.

And so ended his twenty year career in the Navy. Once discharged, he wondered what to do. First he looked up his brother Jack, and found him to be sheriff in Laramie, Wyoming.

Very well. Wyoming was as good as any other place to decide what to do with the rest of his life. At least, unlike others in the same situation, Dane McRavy had no regrets. He'd lived his life to the fullest and he was proud of his years in military service.

* * *

VIVIAN SINCLAIR

To find out about new releases and about other books written by Vivian Sinclair visit her website at VivianSinclairBooks.com or follow her on the Author page at Amazon, Facebook at Vivian Sinclair Books, or on GoodReads.com

Maitland Legacy, A Family Saga Trilogy - western contemporary romances

Book 1 – Lost In Wyoming – Lance's story

Book 2 – Moon Over Laramie – Tristan's story

Book 3 – Christmas In Cheyenne – Raul's story

Wyoming Christmas Trilogy – western contemporary romances

Book 1 – Footprints In The Snow – Tom's story

Book 2 – A Visitor For Christmas – Brianna's story

Book 3 – Trapped On The Mountain – Chris' story

Summer Days In Wyoming Trilogy - western contemporary romances

Book 1 – A Ride In The Afternoon

Book 2 – Fire At Midnight

Book 3 – Misty Meadows At Dawn

Seattle Rain series - women's fiction novels

Book 1 - A Walk In The Rain

Book 2 – Rain, Again!

Book 3 – After The Rain

Virginia Lovers Trilogy - contemporary romance:

Book 1 – Alexandra's Garden

Book 2 – Ariel's Summer Vacation

Book 3 – Lulu's Christmas Wish

A Guest At The Ranch – western contemporary romance

Storm In A Glass Of Water – a small town story

95026440R00153

Made in the USA
Columbia, SC
03 May 2018